The Stories of the Great Steppe

The Anthology of Modern Kazakh Literature

First Edition

Edited by Dr. Rafis Abazov
Columbia University

Translated by Sergey Levchin
and Ilya Bernshtein

Bassim Hamadeh, CEO and Publisher
Michael Simpson, Vice President of Acquisitions
Jamie Giganti, Managing Editor
Jess Busch, Graphic Design Supervisor
Melissa Barcomb, Acquisitions Editor
Sarah Wheeler, Senior Project Editor
Stephanie Sandler, Licensing Associate

ISBN: 978-1-62131-837-8 (pbk)

www.cognella.com   800-200-3908

Recent Praise for
The Stories of the Great Steppe

"The anthology edited by Professor Rafis Abazov appeals to all students and professionals alike offering a very readable and a well-thought out collection of the best literary works from Kazakhstan. This is an engaging text where readers travel intellectually and literary to the Kazakh land and are richly rewarded for their journey."

Prof. Robert J. Guttman
Johns Hopkins University

"*Stories of the Great Steppe* is an important milestone in the building of a post-Soviet Kazakh national identity. The anthology of prose and poetry from Kazakh authors of the Soviet and post-Soviet era draws from deep levels of the Kazakh psyche. This remarkable collection of writings, ably selected by Columbia University professor, Rafis Abazov, conveys to the Western reader a palpable sense of how the Kazakh peoples were shaped and sculpted by the expansive geography of the steppes, whether living on it as a common horse rustler or dreaming of those who soared over it (Yuri Gagarin), but inevitably returning to it. Astute foreign investors will search for a key that opens their eyes to understanding what makes a different society tick. American business people will do well to peruse the pages of this volume and unlock the new vistas it holds for those who wish to build lasting relationships in this increasingly important land."

William Veale, Executive Director
U.S.–Kazakhstan Business Association

"Through its broad-ranging selections of post-World War II prose and poetry, this anthology opens up to readers of English a new world of literature from Central Asia's multilingual and multicultural land of Kazakhstan. Abazov's critical introductory essay summarizes the breadth and depth of subject-matters and cultural influences in the literary traditions from which these very appealing selections derive. The glossary and bibliography add to the book's usefulness for courses on Eurasian culture and the culture of Kazakhstan in particular. The works presented defy any stereotype of simplicity, or of Kazakhstan's secondary, provincial status within a broader Soviet literary system. We find here amidst expected influences such as Socialist Realism deeply differing perspectives, sometimes seeming to reference a unique or highly localized Kazakh cultural milieu, and at other times presenting varied Kazakh images of heroism, of tradition and modernity, of social justice and its opposite, within a fully global context. This selection of Kazakhstan's remarkable output of twentieth-century literature will be of great interest to social and art historians as well as those interested in literature. Surely all readers will appreciate the rich and revealing narratives found here."

Paul Michael Taylor, Ph.D., Director,
Asian Cultural History Program, Smithsonian Institution

Table of Contents

PART I: PROSE

Acknowledgments

By Dr. Rafis Abazov

For many years I have participated in cultural and public diplomacy events around the world, in the process discovering the importance of culture in building bridges between nations and in developing a better understanding of the world among students. In today's world, students and scholars who would like to learn about countries like Kazakhstan can access good collections in public and university libraries. Indeed, the libraries in many research universities in the USA host large collections of books, albums, and media publications from Kazakhstan; however, most of them have never been translated into English. Yet there is huge interest in this country. My colleagues and I have hosted several prominent intellectuals, poets, and writers from Kazakhstan, and we have found there is a great interest in the modern Kazakh cultural universe in the USA, as well as in other developed countries. In consequence, after many discussions we came up with the idea of publishing a comprehensive collection of the poems of Olzhas Suleimenov. This was a great success.

We then decided it was time for a next step—to publish a concise anthology of modern Kazakh literature in English that would serve as a short introduction to the contemporary Kazakh literary universe. I began research for the anthology several years ago. To our surprise, we soon discovered that a project along these lines has never been done before.

The *Anthology of Modern Kazakh Literature* emerged from several years of intensive consultation and research on cultural and social development in Kazakhstan. Some initial findings were gathered while I was working on the books *The Culture and Customs of the Central Asian Republics* (2007) and *Green Desert: The Life and Poetry of Olzhas Suleimenov* (2011). During the last two or three years I also asked many people around me—my students, colleagues, and friends as well as researchers and readers from many parts of the world—about the content that they would like to see in English. My colleagues and I have had a long series of discussions on authors who should be translated and introduced to the American audience. After many rounds of consultation, we decided to focus on works of those writers and poets who have been writing from non-Western perspectives and who have greatly contributed to the intellectual discourse in Kazakhstan in the post-World War Two period.

The visit of Olzhas Suleimenov to New York, his public reading at Columbia University in fall of 2009, and the discovery of a large number of his fans and followers, who came to meet him from many cities and towns around the United States and Canada, gave me confidence in the success of the *Anthology* project. This event strengthened my belief that there is a need for a serious translation of Suleimenov's work. I was delighted that the University Readers Publishing House and especially Melissa Barcomb, Senior Field Acquisitions Editor, provided enthusiastic support for this book project, and a commitment to seeing it through the stages leading to its publication. My deep gratitude also goes to Sarah Wheeler, Project Editor at Cognella, Inc., who worked on this project with me from the beginning.

The *Anthology* was prepared as an introduction to the literature of Kazakhstan since 1945, for the US. audience. Unfortunately, very few works of contemporary Kazakh writers have been translated into English and other European languages during the last twenty years. I feel it is very important to fill that gap. For this publication, about a dozen pieces in prose and verse were selected. I am fully aware that this is a very, very small part of the modern literature of Kazakhstan, and I hope that many more such translations will be made available to us in the future.

This book has become possible only through the invaluable contributions of many people. My Kazakh colleagues generously shared their thoughts about Kazakh literature and the most prominent names in the contemporary intellectual discourse in that country and the Eurasian region. I especially appreciate the help and assistance I received from the librarians with whom I worked while I was researching this volume, notably including Robert H. Davis of the Slavic Collection of Columbia University Library. Several colleagues and friends agreed to read and discuss the manuscript and translations during early stages of the preparation of this work. Numerous conversations and debates with scholars, poets, and critics at various academic and non-academic conventions enriched my knowledge about the peculiarities of cultural development in Kazakhstan and about modern Kazakh literature.

Some young scholars and then my students in Almaty city—Aiman Imentai, Andrei Khasbulatov, Moldir Nurpeis, and many others in my Global Classroom Program—helped with the background research. Dr. Murat Auezov, Jamilya Sembi and their colleagues at the Mukhtar Auezov Foundation agreed to meet with me to discuss various aspects of modern Kazakh literature. The president of Al Farabi Kazakh National University, Prof. Galymkair Mutanov, hosted me at Al Farabi KazNU, providing an intellectual environment for my work. The first-vice-president of Al Farabi Kazakh National University, Prof. Mukhametbetkali Burkitbayev and his team, provided me all possible support and consultations while I was researching on the book and travelling intensively around the country. Several faculty members from Al Farabi Kazakh National University, including Prof. Galiya Ibrayeva, Prof. Karlyga Misayeva, and some others shared their research papers on topics related to this publication. Ms. Naomi Caffee, a Ph.D. student at UCLA specializing in Russophone Central Asian literature and Olzhas Suleimenov's literary heritage, kindly read early versions of the work and contributed valuable comments and suggestions in the preparation of this manuscript.

My particular thanks to Prof. Ualikhan Kalimzhanov, Director of the Mukhtar Auezov Institute of Literature and Art, and his colleagues from that institute including Svetlana Ananieva and Mukan Amangeldi. These and several other scholars provided support to this project during early stage, including Zifa Auezova, Bakhytzhan Kanapianov, Seit Kaskabasov, Arystanbek Mukhamediuly, Duisenbek Nakipov, Nurlan Sanjar, Zhaken Taimagambetov, and Zaituna Zhandosova. Prof. Ualikhan Kalimzhanov was also instrumental in selecting the prose and poetry works for the Anthology.

I would like to thank Sergey Levchin and Ilya Bernstein for their tireless efforts and commitment to the project.

I would also like to express my special gratitude to then-Ambassador Extraordinary and Plenipotentiary of the Republic of Kazakhstan to the USA, Mr. Erlan Idrissov,[1] and all his colleagues for helping me to gain access to publications about the culture and literature of Kazakhstan and for assisting in arranging several meetings with prominent cultural figures and intellectuals from Kazakhstan.

Rafis Abazov (PhD)
Columbia University, USA

Visiting Professor
Al Farabi Kazakh National University, Kazakhstan

---

1 In September 2012 Mr. Erlan Idrissov has been appointed as Kazakhstan's foreign minister and transferred to Astana, Kazakhstan.

Foreword

By Ambassador Erlan Idrissov

As an ambassador of the Republic of Kazakhstan, I strongly believe that our writers and poets are my colleagues—they are the greatest cultural ambassadors for my country. With their poems, stories, and novels they contribute to citizens' diplomacy: building bridges between ordinary people in a greater understanding of everyday life, culture, and thought; adding to discourses on a wide variety of issues; deciding what is relevant to our society yesterday, today, and tomorrow; and building a better understanding of the place of Kazakhstan in the modern world.

Therefore, it is my great pleasure today to introduce the first ever publication in the USA of an anthology of modern Kazakh literature. These stories and poems have been carefully selected by the editor with help from leading scholars in Kazakhstan, including the Mukhtar Auezov Institute of Literature and Art, the Mukhtar Auezov Foundation, and Al Farabi Kazakh National University. Through a series of discussions and meetings they have brought together a comprehensive overview of modern Kazakh literature since World War Two. Of course, the Kazakh literature of this seventy-year period is much richer than even a thousand such volumes could accommodate, and it is represented by hundreds if not thousands of interesting and intellectually stimulating works. Unfortunately, only a relatively small number of these works have made it into the collection.

The pieces selected for this Anthology were created by the most talented poets and writers in Kazakhstan in the post-World War Two period and reflect one of the most decisive pages of the history of my native land. It was the era of the 1950s and 60s, when the young generation of our citizens believed in the unlimited power of progress, modernization, and technology, and it was they who built the foundations of the modern Kazakh economy and state. One example will serve to illustrate the contrasts and changes in Kazakh society during that era: just imagine—hundreds of young Kazakhs travelled on horses and camels to a remote area in southern Kazakhstan to build the technological marvel of the twentieth century, the Baikonur Space Center. In the open desert, where only the wild wind and cold moonlight had commanded the sand dunes and rocky hills for millennia, those young people together with their colleagues from all over the world built a modern space station. This space station—the largest on Earth during the twentieth century—sent more spaceships to the sky than any other station in the world. Admiration of the power of human intellect and progress was reflected in Olzhas Suleimenov's poems of that era, and in Suleimenov's words "… ignited the fire of your youth."

The life of Kazakh society during the first decades in the post-WWII era, however, was also full of social contrasts and social changes. On several occasions in reading western scholarly works I have come across a simplified account of life in our society during that time, an overly simplistic portrayal flattening the lives of our people under single ideological slogans. In reality, the life of Kazakh society, as in many neighboring states, was much richer and more complex. People had developed their own ideas and thoughts about the social and cultural changes and about political development, and hotly debated them in small circles or intellectual and literary clubs. These lively discourses were well reflected in several stories and poems selected for this Anthology.

Like people in all other societies around the world, rebellious youth and intellectuals in Kazakhstan fiercely debated many issues, from literary forms and trends to cultural and political issues, and from the interactions of traditional nomadic values with the forces of modernity and globalization to the meaning of modernism and post-modernism in the local Central Asian context. I know from my American colleagues how intensive were the discourses in the American society and literary world in the 1960s and 70s, and I am confident to claim that similar trends and intensity of exchanges could be seen in the intellectual circles in my country. Of course, the culture and political system and political environment had a significant impact on the ways in which our intellectuals—journalists, scholars, and writers—managed to present or hide in Aesopian language their thoughts and ideas. But it is inevitable in all corners of the world that the historical, economic, and political environment asserts its own influence on modern discourses. Though, I have to say that in our country in those days the cost of free alternative views and expressions was sometimes quite high—punishment for free thinking in Soviet society could be quite severe. Some writers did indeed become conformists. Yet, the fact that even in this restrictive environment our intellectuals were brave enough to find ways to express their thoughts is admirable. Not all people agreed with the changes around them, and in literary ways they expressed their thoughts and dreams on societal ideals, searching for the golden centuries of Kazakh society in our history.

Kazakhs have a beautiful proverb: "Words of a true *akyn* [poet] can warm you better than the sun." I hope that this Anthology of Kazakh literature will warm the hearts of its readers.

Erlan Idrissov

Ambassador Extraordinary and Plenipotentiary of the Republic of Kazakhstan to the United States. He was appointed as the Foreign Minister of Kazakhstan on September 28, 2012.

Foreword

Kazakh Literature and Modernity
КАЗАХСКАЯ ЛИТЕРАТУРА И СОВРЕМЕННОСТЬ

By Ualikhan Kalizhanov
Director of Mukhtar Auezov Institute of Literature and Art

Kazakh literature is an organic part of world culture. Our literature is a mirror of our culture and our society, and occupies an important place in the intellectual discourse in our country. In adapting to the new social and cultural reality, Kazakh literature strengthens its contacts with the literatures of the West and the East. Trends in the literary world of today include creating an atmosphere of genuine freedom of creativity, overcoming rigid sociological descriptiveness, discussing previously taboo topics (national theme/reinterpreting the real history of the country) and different ideological and aesthetic concepts. Contemporary writers can portray reality in all its complexity within this broadened creative scope. Kazakh literature continues the classical traditions of the past and takes them to a new level, significantly expanding the boundaries of creative interpretations and studies.

At the initiative of President Nursultan Nazarbayev of the Republic of Kazakhstan we are successfully implementing the State program "Cultural Heritage." The program covers a number of important and wide-ranging measures to preserve, study, and promote the best examples of the artistic culture of the Kazakh people. The underlying concept of the unique nature of the project is the thesis that national literature is important in forming national identity. In recent years the works of repressed writers and previously unpublished examples of folklore have been widely printed.

Independence has opened up new horizons, creating optimal conditions for the development of the literary process and for identifying the role and importance of literature in the development of a modern national identity. The epochal nature of the events of modern history has endowed our national literature with a new face and new features, clearly demonstrated in the intensity of the development of literature in the country today. Contemporary Kazakh literature is characterized by its variety of themes, relaxed manner of writing, and stylistic richness. Difficult situations, spiritual and moral quests, individual resistance to political and ideological pressures, and the problems of the Kazakh village are the focus of the greatest Kazakh artists of the word. Modernity as a categorical phenomenon represents a paradigm shift, changing the entire structure of a work of art.

Alongside the modern theme, history remains a dominant theme in Kazakh literature. Each work of the greatest masters of artistic expression is a special world that has been put together and organized. It lives according to the laws of creativity. National writers do not fit in well-defined traditional boundaries of trends and literary movements. Gabit Musrepov and his generation were a mirror of Kazakh literature of the twentieth century and its rich artistic heritage. A great master of artistic expression, Musrepov headed a brilliant group of Kazakh writers and playwrights. They reflected an era of great social change, and embodied it in bright national characters created with an adept hand.

An organic component of Kazakh prose is mythology. The popular culture, songs, legends, stories, and myths of the Kazakh people have stimulated interest in archaic and mythological motifs. Many authors have used this "mythology of world view" to reconstruct a picture of the past, as if warning their contemporaries of rash decisions and actions. Lessons of the past should not be forgotten.

Novelists entice the modern reader with new interpretations of history, and new thinking about the meaning of time. Modern authors often act as researchers, leading independent forays in search of truth and re-conceptualizing the lessons of history. These re-envisionings reveal new narrative possibilities and serve as the dominant criterion of ideological and structural organization of the Kazakh historical novel.

Modernism and postmodernism are most tangible in Kazakh literature: the poetics of compromise, psychology, and drama; overcoming spatial and temporal boundaries; search for ideals; stylistic features as a manifestation of the intertext; changes in syntax; etc. Deepening the psychology of modern Kazakh prose leads to expanding the boundaries of poetry and style, enriching and transforming narrative in the novel system. Internal monologues and dialogues, quasi-direct speeches of characters, are increasingly applied in the structures of novels and stories, in an extroversion of feeling and thought.

Psychological analysis enriches the content of the Kazakh novel, realistically reproducing the dynamics of the development and improvement of the spiritual world of the people. Traditional visual forms incorporate new ways of creative thinking to explain the diversity of the Kazakh novel.

The poets of Kazakhstan can be appreciated in the dimensions of their poetic and stylistic approach, melodic intonation, and rhythmic features. Kazakh poetry is an interesting phenomenon in terms of genre and stylistic originality and conceptual and thematic content. A peculiar aspect of the literary process of Kazakhstan is the work of writers and poets who write in different languages.

Russian-language writers represent a broad literary trend that emerged at the border and the junction of the two cultures and literatures. These writers help to build "a bridge between the two cultures and guide interaction" (Olzhas Suleimenov). Importantly, their work represents a fundamental move beyond a single national culture and literature. Representatives of Kazakh literature, such as poet and writer Olzhas Suleimenov, are accepted as a part of modern world culture. At the same time, the work of each of the national writers and poets creates a national image of the world. Co-existence (in the words of Suleimenov) becomes the determining factor in their prose, which depicts the evolution of the feelings, thoughts, and experiences of the characters, the intense inner life. It redefines aesthetic ideals, the revision of values against immutable universal criteria.

The era of integration and search for innovative solutions can be equated with realism in art, in which is inherent a heightened attention to the specific qualities of the individual, and the dialectic of the soul. Our literary artists increasingly win the attention of society by creating realistic images of contemporary or historical figures, updating and perfecting the concept of identity.

Kazakh literature, in which the integration of a world-scale artistic process is obvious, is of strategic importance for the sustainable adoption of the national identity, intercultural dialogue, and the strengthening of the spiritual image of our country in the world.

Of course, not all the words of well-known Kazakh artists are included in this anthology. I believe the time is coming when the American reader will seek to know more about the literature of Kazakhstan and our cultural heritage.

Introduction

By Dr. Rafis Abazov

When I talk to my students about the culture of Central Asia I try to make engaging and enlightening comparisons. As I begin talking about Central Asian culture I often tell them they are about to discover things that are completely new to them: they are about to open a window that looks out on a different galaxy. Some of what they see may seem familiar at first glance—built, after all, on the same humanistic structures—but I always suggest that they stop for a moment to think and look more closely: beneath and inside familiar forms and shapes lies an immensely different experience. Contemporary literature is a substantial and infinitely revealing part of this distinctive universe. Indeed, this is a unique universe of people who lived in the never ending steppe for millennia and who built their worldviews by looking both at the beauty of the land where they put their *yurts*, nomadic felt tents, and by looking beyond horizons for new ideas and new opportunities.

There are different and competing views on the Kazakh literature of the post-World War Two era. One group stresses how it has developed under strong Russian and Soviet influence, pointing out that it has incorporated and developed only the major themes of the Russian and Soviet literary heritage and has followed the trend of Socialist realism. Social realism has been, according to these scholars, the overriding formational influence on modern Kazakh writers, poets, and journalists, and has therefore heavily infused Kazakh literature with ideologically motivated topics and themes. Thus, this school of literary criticism claims, contemporary Kazakh literature should be viewed exclusively in the context of Soviet literature. Little Kazakh literature was translated into the Western languages between the 1950s and the 1980s, with most of the translations and publications being the work of the "Progress" Soviet Publishing House in Moscow. Even though very few published works from Kazakhstan actually had an ideological flavor, mere association with the

Soviet publishing house often led to the perception of their being ideologically motivated. Therefore, scholars who study the literature of the Eurasian region rarely focus on the Kazakh literature of the post-World War Two period, and very few research works find their way to the pages of Western academic journals. The post-Soviet Kazakh literature also remains largely *terra incognita* in the West, for scholars as for the general public, as it is seldom made available by Western publishing companies. There is, of course, a much larger body of research literature on this period, but very often this literary criticism evolves around the same few topics, such as national identity, nation-state building, and some other aspects of the modern Kazakh literature.

The other group of literary critics calls for a more nuanced assessment of the literary production of modern Kazakh writers. They agree that during the Soviet era between the 1950s and 1980s the popular culture, literature included, was heavily influenced by Soviet ideological perceptions, censorship, and the social realism approach. Yet they point out that, firstly, there were changes over time. The "thaw" of the 1960s had a long-lasting effect on subsequent generations of writers, poets, and journalists who looked for inspiration not only in the West and Western and Russian culture, but also in the traditional culture of Central Asia—not only in modernity and modernism, but also in traditionalist values of their own localities. Secondly, with the rise of national identity and national culture in the twentieth century more Kazakh writers and poets have begun thinking and discussing and often calling to rediscover the roots of modern Kazakh culture not only in the "West" but also in the mystic "Orient." These "roots" could be found in the heritage of Turkic nomadic civilization with its unique perception of mother nature and cosmology of nomads manifested in the peculiar view of the power and responsibility of the individual being connected to the commander of the circles of life (powerful Yer-Suu) and weaved whimsically with the influential thoughts of Sufi thinkers who preached in the Eurasian steppe for centuries. Thirdly, the Kazakh intelligentsia, like those in Eastern and Central Europe, had grown accustomed to century-long cat and mouse games with the censors and the state bureaucrats. Like generations of writers in Imperial Russia of the nineteenth century, they accepted the Procrustean bed of censorship, but they filled their works with allegories, symbols, and surreptitious—and sometimes not so surreptitious— messages in order to get around the strict rules and restrictions and to express their thoughts and ideas. These critics, therefore, would have us avoid clichés and generalizations, and carefully examine the rich and wonderful heritage of the Kazakh literature of this era. After all, many writers, poets, and intellectuals endeavored in their works to reflect and discuss the massive social changes and transformations and to deal—in their own ways—with the most common themes of that era, thus contributing to intellectual discourses in their own home country and in their region.

It is not necessarily for a nomad to travel physically around the world, although actual travel between different localities is an important part of his nature. Sometimes s/he moves around in the thoughts and the movement consists of a spiritual search for the meaning of life and one's place in this universe. Maybe this is one of the reasons, reflected in the Kazakh literature and manifested in many literary works, that Kazakh literature often invents and focuses on these travels and these explorations. One of the main characteristics of a nomad is his or her curiosity and desire to explore both the locality and the universe around him or her. A nomad is interested in learning, traveling, experimenting, and exploring in an attempt to build these explored knowledge and feelings into his or her mosaic of the personal perception of the world around an exploring nomad. This might be one of the main reasons that characters both in prose and poetry in Kazakhstan are often on the move, both on the personal move in exploring themselves and their relations with the people and the world around them and on the actual move—exploring new localities and meeting new places.

Another popular motif in the cultural symbolism of a nomad and nomadic life is the relation with nature. Here a human being is a part of the universe equal to all living creatures overlooked and handled by the mother earth. However, s/he has one significant feature: a human being has a power and ability to make a difference—it is in his power to make this world a better place or worse. Yet a nomad is not entirely independent from the nature around him or her—the mother earth might and indeed would come after a nomad if s/he makes mistakes and destroys nature, especially animals around him. From this perception of the habitat and the world comes one of the interesting and quite common features in the Kazakh literature—the ability of a person to talk to animals and trees or to simply to share his or her thoughts, emotions, worries, and happiness. At certain points in Kazakh literature, especially in the 1950s and 1960s, a large group of writers and poets reinterpreted the traditional nomadic relations with the mother earth and focused on conquering mother earth and building a new technocratic society. In this technocratic society people were free of "superstitions" and were using new technologies (large factories) and new relations (brought together into collective farms (kolkhoz)) to conquer mother earth and build modernity—a "modern" world for a nomad free of restrictive relations with the mother earth. Yet there always were groups of writers and poets who opposed those views and interpretations of the life of a nomad. In their works they called for respecting and remembering the traditional nomadic philosophy of life and reminded that mother earth would always come after them and attempt to restore the balance (or in modern language, eco-balance) by punishing those who destroyed nature.

These discourses and hot debates between "modernists" and "traditionalists" manifested different competing concepts of a nomad-hero. Both camps turned to a traditional motif in nomadic culture and folklore—a motif of a hero, but reinterpreted and reinvented in very different ways. Both camps were engaged in building collective positive characters for the hero and borrowing ideas from competing camps to build a character of an anti-hero. On one side of the ring was a hero who presented a power derived from modernity—logic, knowledge, and the ability to control emotions and reject old traditions and "superstitions" and even to sacrifice his love for his cause. On the other side of the ring was a traditional hero, often derived from traditional legends and from folklore. Like the authors of the classic heroic literature of Europe, the twentieth century "traditionalists" often romanticized a medieval knight or invented brave modern social warrior—a person with superior personal values: honesty and bravery and devotion to his love. The nomad-knight in Kazakh literature, like his counterparts in Western classic literature, is a manifestation and symbol of the highest quality in friendship and in building his personal relations with loved ones, yet he is full of emotions and superstitions that often lead him to make personal and social mistakes.

This "traditionalist" school of Kazakh writers—both during the Soviet and during the post-Soviet era—turned for inspiration to the history of Kazakh land and Kazakh tribes, especially to the history of the late middle ages and of the modern era before the Bolshevik revolution of 1917.

2. Kazakh Literature and Modernity

The focal point of modern Kazakh literature has been the issue of modernity. The Kazakh intellectuals have dealt with the rapidly changing would around them, as the traditional slow-moving pre-industrial society has been rapidly changing around them in an uncatchable speed. These changes have impacted not only everyday life, political and social relations, but also culture, values, special relations, and world views.

And these complex changes led to intricate clashes between old and new, the values from the East and West, deeply localized community-based cultures and cultural perceptions with highly internationalized and globalized perceptions of modernity and the modern world. On the top of it, deeply conservative perceptions of family values and interpersonal relations based on the tribal notions of honor and honesty clashed with very different notions of modern family, society, and social relations. And Kazakh intellectuals have thought to discuss the impact of modernity at individual psychological levels, to explore family conflicts and the changing nature of social relations between generations, reflecting these changes, challenges, and clashes in artistic ways.

On the top of it, the post-World War Two era was the era of the rise of mass literature and mass readership. Very quickly—within a couple of decades—Kazakh society turned from a society of mass illiteracy to one of the most reading nations in the world.

The modern literature of the twentieth century reflected complex changes in Kazakh society.[1] It bridged the gap between the nomadic oral heritage and new literature, which experimented with European models—"new" forms, especially in prose. The literary heritage of this era is an intricate reflection of these changes.

In general, Kazakh literature, like Central Asian Soviet-era literature, revolved around three major themes—the revolt against old traditions and prejudices, the search for and establishment of social justice, and an awakening of a new hero and rebel spirit in the ordinary person. These themes were developed against a background of dramatic polarization wrought by the Bolshevik revolution in Kazakh society, and the extraordinary social, cultural, and political changes instigated by the Soviet system, which radically altered the lives of every person in the region. The Schwarzenegger of Kazakh Soviet literature, however, was not of a kind readily adaptable into today's Hollywood "action-hero." His main mission was to change himself and people around him. His rebellion was against social injustice, traditional ways of life, rich and oppressive lords (*bais*), or restrictive ancient rituals. Also, he challenged the age-old conception of family and personal honor and their associated codes of revenge and forgiveness.

The social changes in the literary and intellectual world in Kazakhstan made a huge impact on the development of the literature and criticism. The old social barriers were removed and many talented individual from all kinds of backgrounds—working class, peasants, ethnic and religious minorities—received an opportunity and often were encouraged to reflect their personal experiences and the experiences of the people around them. Young Kazakh authors actively experimented in new genres, styles, and themes by learning from classic Western and Russian literature and poetry, as many of them translated those works into local languages by themselves. All these changes significantly undermined influences of the classical Kazakh oral traditional heritage, building favor for a completely new literary universe, though many poets and writers frequently turned to the classic Kazakh oral traditions for inspirations and themes.

Yet creativity in the Soviet system had its limits. The Soviet system did not tolerate criticism or deviation from the ruling party line. For many decades the government imposed a strait jacket of rules in the form of the "socialist realist approach in literature."[2] Socialist realism stipulated "truthful, historically concrete reflection of reality in its revolutionary development."[3]

Like many Soviet writers of that era, Kazakh authors wrote about building the "new Soviet life" through the *kolkhozes* and industrial enterprises. But what distinguished the Kazakh writers was that they dramatized and complicated these stock themes by adding new local flavor and out of the ordinary nuances, and they represented the culturally distinctive patriarchal ways of Kazakh life and religious backwardness as qualities in need of modern redemption. A typical cliché in the writing of this period was the depiction of newcomers (often urban educated and modern) as people of superior moral and spiritual power who helped the influential local characters to abandon the old (and "wrong") ways of life and "discover" the irresistible power of the Soviet ideology and "culture."

Between the 1950s and the 1990s the major literary themes have been Soviet patriotism and World War Two (also called the Great Patriotic War (1941–1945)). The war had a huge impact on Kazakh society, as this war was depicted and perceived as a defense of the motherland from the powerful enemy who threatened the very existence of the society and the country. The suffering of ordinary people from hardship of the war era and the bravery of those tens of thousands of young people who fought thousands of miles away stimulated the comparison with the past history of Kazakh society and the Kazakh steppe and interest in historical novels for many decades. Some Kazakh writers also turned to historical issues, writing monumental historical novels. Various dramatic and decisive pages from Kazakh history were illustrated by Iliyas Esemberlin in the trilogy *Koshpendiler* (Nomads) and *Altyn Orda* (Golden Horde), by Mukhtar Auezov (1897–1961) in his monumental four-volume novel *Abai* and *Abai Zholy* (The Path of Abai), by Abdizhamil Nurpeisov in the trilogy *Kan men ter* (Blood and Sweat), by Abish Kekilbayev in *Abylai Khan*, by Saken Zhunisov in *Akhan Sere* and *Amanai men Zamanai* (Amanai and Zamanai), by Anuar Alimzhanov in *Makhambettin zhebesi* (The Arrow of Makhambet), and by others.

Probably the most popular genre in Kazakh literature has been short novels and short stories, as this format found mass readership through publications in literary newspapers, in cultural and literary magazines, and in small American-style take-to-the-beach format inexpensive collections of short stories. The best works of that era focused on changing relationships in small close-knit communities in remote areas. They described how difficulties and sufferings helped people to overcome family, tribal, and communal differences and relayed Romeo and Juliet-style romantic stories about young people whose love helped them to overcome the prejudice of old social traditions, vendettas, or social and cultural barriers. Importantly, during this era a new common character emerged in Central Asian literature; this time he was a local hero returned home to a small town or city—the Kazakh equivalent of Alabama or Montana—bringing a whole new universe with him or her after experiencing a "new" life in a completely different "real Soviet" environment.

Among the writers of short stories who won huge followings and commanded large audiences were Gabit Musrepov (1902–1985), with his short stories and essays with picturesque depiction of the life in Kazakh *auils* (villages); Abish Kekilbayev (1939-), who mastered romanticizing the Kazakh steppe; Rollan Seisenbayev (1946-) who produced interesting short stories about the youth; Oralkhan Bokeev (1943–1993), who idealized the simple life of people living in the countryside and the beauty of Kazakh nature; Tulen Abdikov (1942-), who mastered short stories and novels about people and nature; Mukhtar Magauin (1940-), whose short stories attracted attention by depicting the relations between people and natural world; and Muagali Makatayev (1931–1976), whose poems attracted attention by depicting and romanticizing simple life in Kazakh *auil.*

The life of Olzhas Suleimenov—Kazakh poet, writer, and intellectual—is a good example.

Olzhas Suleimenov (1936-). While a student at Kazakh State University he began to write poetry. In 1958–1959 he attended the Gorky Literary Institute (Moscow). In 1959 he published his first collection of poems in Moscow. From 1961 to 1975 he worked variously as a journalist, an editor of the literary journal *Prostor,* an editor at the studios of *Kazakh-film,* and in administration for the Kazakh Union of Writers. His poem *Zemlia poklonis cheloveku* (The Globe bow to a man!) (1961) brought him wide recognition. In 1975 Suleimenov published his book *Az-i-ia,*[4] a historical-philosophical essay on Turkic historical destiny.[5] In it he explored the history of the interaction between nomads (Turks) and settlers (Slavs) and the place of the Kazakhs in the historical development of Eurasia. The publication was condemned by Moscow's policy makers as "nationalistic," and the book was confiscated and banned until 1989. Suleimenov became one of the most prominent Kazakhi dissidents of the 1970s, and only the personal intervention of the Kazakh first secretary, Dinmuhammed Kunaev, saved him from imprisonment. *Az-i-ia* won him nationwide recognition in Kazakhstan and a reputation as the "opener of difficult issues in the national history." After political rehabilitation, he worked in various positions with the Union of Writers. He became one of the most influential writers in Kazakhstan in the 1980s. His active public life in the 1980s won him a reputation as the "voice of the Kazakh intelligentsia":

> A word—[is] a leisurely reflection of a human deed.
> The height, depth and colors are begot by the tongue.
> Reflected in the words are a sip,
> And a strike of a blow,
> And a smile,
> A sound of hooves through the aeon,
> And incline of a weighed-down vine.[6]

In the 1970s and 1980s mainstream writers continued to explore the crucial social issues surrounding the development of Soviet society. During this time Central Asian literature was more in line with popular Soviet themes, as many writers depicted the life of large collectives, where innovators and enthusiasts struggled against opportunists and conservatives. Yet some Central Asian writers ventured away from propaganda and the Socialist Realism theme and began exploring such forbidden issues as the rise of nationalism or anti-colonial struggles, or they simply revised and even challenged state-impose dogmas and ideas, especially official Russia-centric interpretations of history and cultural development. For example, Kazakh poet Olzhas Sulemenov, in his book *Az-i-ia,* turned to the traditional issues—the history of nomadic steppe—radically departing from the ruling party-approved interpretation of the conflicts of those periods and paving the way towards creating alternative historical accounts.

The quality of Soviet-era literature was very uneven. Even Soviet literary critics recognized the existence of works they deemed "primitive with no artistic merit," having "clichéd characters ... with stereotype heroes" and "vaguely defined" conflicts.[7] The Schwarzenegger of Central Asian literature, like his American "action-hero" counterpart, was predictably a good-looking, politically-correct person, who inevitably challenged bad guys and always won the battle (and often the heart of an attractive woman) despite numerous tricks by his enemies. Yet there were many literary works that reflected upon genuine conflicts between the old and the new, or critically examined the emancipation of women and men from the stultifying restrictions of old tribal, communal, or religious customs. And these, by and large, were the works that the ordinary people were reading. Some extraordinarily talented writers and poets created works that captivated many people in Central Asia and beyond. It is also important to remember that the Soviet authorities were investing heavily in the development of the national identity of the newly created nation-states, and to this end, they sponsored national literature, poetry, art, education, etc. In addition, it must be kept in mind that the Central Asian languages were standardized only in the 1920s and 1930s. Therefore, the national writers and poets of that era were often pioneers who revolutionized national culture by writing not in classical Persian or Turkic but in the languages understandable to ordinary peasants and workers.

3. Post-Soviet Literature

Like the Bolshevik Revolution in 1917, the breakdown of the Soviet Union and breakaway of the Central Asian Republics in 1991 marked an important milestone in the development of the literature of the region. Suddenly many restrictions that had been imposed by the Communist Party *apparatchiks* disappeared. Many topics previously considered politically incorrect became open for public discussion. Also, the national intelligentsia, especially the writers and poets, discovered that they could discuss the development of national culture, national identity, and national history (even its darkest pages) without the approval of Moscow. Interest in national culture and national symbols skyrocketed, and there began a wide public search for hidden symbols and coded anti-colonial sentiments in past and present literature and in the works of the banned writers.

There was also much heated debate about the national literatures of the Soviet and pre-Soviet eras. Many argued that much of Soviet-era literature was so ideologically infested and so superficial in depicting communist-era topics that it did not present any value in the post-Soviet and post-colonial era. At the same time, the Kazakh intelligentsia argued that many authors of the pre-revolutionary and post-revolutionary eras who were banned for their anti-colonial and anti-communist or politically incorrect views should be rehabilitated and given a place in the national cultural heritage. Yet another group argued that the wholesale rejection of Soviet-era literature could not be justified; after all, those works laid the foundation for the national literature. Those writers also reflected the realities of everyday life, the depth of the political and social divides in the societies, and the confrontation between representatives of different generations and different social groups. These debates hit the pages of national newspapers, magazines, and literary journals and sparked lively polemics about the historical development of art, literature, and poetry.

While intellectuals were busy reevaluating the achievements and faults of their national literature, and the ways in which to respond to the changing world, the world itself arrived at their doorsteps in the form of crises that struck the literary circles on many fronts. Kazakhstan's government significantly cut its previously generous subsidies to publishing houses, writers unions, book clubs, and individual authors. It was now up to the market or rich philanthropists to decide which authors could publish and survive in this very unstable environment. At the same time, the reading audience was shrinking at catastrophic rates, with recession, poverty, and unemployment affecting more than three-quarters of the population. Many people, even professionals—teachers, researchers, doctors, lawyers—could no longer afford to buy books. And most importantly, many writers themselves, especially of the younger generation, failed to pen significant pieces worthy of wide public attention, as many intellectuals really struggled to capture the essence and impact of social and cultural changes around them and to come up with captivating and appealing pieces.

All of these factors engendered pessimistic themes and an emphasis on crises at the personal, communal, or societal level. The verses of Kazakh poet Konysbai Ebil to some degree reflect this trend:

I don't care
If it is bazaar or market:
If you have knowledge—show it;
I can't define anyone as the "enemy of the nation" [anymore]
And there is also no one who has concerns about the people.[8]

Yet, despite these problems, some authors managed to continue to write, producing some interesting works. Paradoxically, the call to return to national roots was not realized in a grand revival of pre-modern genres and styles, although there was increasing public interest in traditional heroic epics, legends, *tamasha* (humor and satiric stories), etc. Many old works were republished with new and extensive commentaries. Most contemporary authors continue the modern Western traditions in writing novels, short stories, poems, and polemical essays on various social, cultural and political issues.

It would not be an exaggeration to say that Kazakh literature has been at a crossroads ever since independence in 1991. Many factors account for the slow and painful transition. The most noticeable trend is that the reading audience is much smaller than in the past and is slowly shrinking further. Although living standards have been gradually improving, many social groups have been struggling to adapt to the new economic reality.

The second important trend is the fragmentation and polarization of society. Social groups are stratified not only in terms of income. There can be seen the emergence of significant differences in living standards between urban and rural areas and growing differences and even rivalries between representatives of different provinces that begin in politics and extend to all other aspects of life. There is also a growing gap between the secular intelligentsia and the religiously oriented intelligentsia, and significant differences in values and lifestyles between people who grew up and were educated during the Soviet era and the post-Soviet period.

Notes

1. There is no precisely defined date for the transition between the pre-colonial and colonial eras in Central Asian cultural history, as the region was conquered by the Russian Empire step by step over several decades.
2. For a comprehensive review of the development of Central Asian literature during the Imperial Russian and Soviet eras, see: Edward Allworth, "The Changing Intellectual and Literary Community" and "The Focus on Literature," in Edward Allworth (ed.), *Central Asia: 130 Years of Russian Dominance: A Historical Overview*, Third Edition (Durham and London: Duke University Press, 1994), pp. 349–433.

3. *Ustav Souza pisatelei SSSR* [The Statute of the Union of Writers of the USSR], (Moscow, 1934).

4. Word play. "Azia" means Asia; and "Az-i-ia" means "Az and me."

5. For detailed discussion, see: Harsha Ram, "Imagining Eurasia: Olzhas Suleimenov's AZ i IA" *Slavic Review.* Volume 60, Number 2, Summer 2001.

6. Translated by S. Peshkin. See: Translated by author. From: Olzhas Suleimenov. *Izbrannoie* [Selected Works]. (Moscow: Khudozhestvenaia literatura, 1986). p. 88.

7. Khalyk Kor-Ogly, *Uzbekskaia literature* [Uzbek Literature] (Moscow: Vys'shaia shkola, 1968), pp. 146–147, 161–162.

8. Konysbai Ebil, "Kekberi kirdi tusume," *Zhas Alash,* No. 60–61, 22 Mamyr, 2004, p. 11.

Part I

Prose

An Ethnographic Tale

By Gabit Musrepov

I t was the third time the district secretary had called me into his office.

"What's going on with you? When are you going down to see about that *auil*? I just don't know what you're waiting for!"

He seemed genuinely troubled, and I didn't try to make excuses. He knew well enough that all this time I had been giving my lectures at the Borovoe Forestry School. He knew—and yet there he was, insisting I set out at once.

A couple of months earlier some half dozen *auils* on the outskirts of our district joined together and became a *kolkhoz*. The whole concept was new. And our district secretary couldn't get his head around the news that the collective stubbornly refused to admit their neighbors from the *auil* of Zhanbyrshi. It just didn't make sense: especially because *that auil*—as we came to call it—sat on the best tracts of land.

From what I could gather, the people of Zhanbyrshi weren't exactly clamoring for collectivization either. Maybe they'd been hearing talk of the *kolkhoz* where everyone wore the same clothes, slept all together under a great communal blanket, got up and went to bed on cue, like it was the army. Evidently if it weren't for "getting up," that sort of life would have suited Zhanbyrshi just fine. Still, what was it that kept them away? If it had been a wealthy *auil*, there wouldn't be much of a mystery. But one of our instructors, who had gone down to see them earlier, found nothing but wretched poverty at every level. And still, he couldn't make any headway with those people. All he heard from them was: "What Allah has ordained, so it shall be."

The district secretary had little confidence in Allah, and that meant I had to interrupt my lectures.

It is a long way from Borovoe to Zhanbyrshi. Naturally, I could have done it on horseback, but I decided to take a cart and ride in comfort on a thick padding of hay. There was only one problem. For some time I had had my eye on a jet-black gelding: four years old, hump-nosed, with a muzzle like the crescent moon. After a few months I couldn't resist it any longer—I bought him. He went like lightning under the saddle, with a grace that immediately separates a good horse from miserable mediocrity. I didn't even mind that he had mange when I bought him. I had cured far worse things.

A real steppe horse is trained for riding, but put him in shafts, and sure as day he'll start jackknifing and turning circles like he's got the staggers. This was just the trip to break my gelding's bad habits. I couldn't manage it alone though, so I invited two of my students from the forestry school to go along for the ride.

We had no shortage of grief along the way, but in the end three young lads proved smarter and stronger than a willful gelding. The sun was going down when we reached the outer tracts of Zhanbyrshi, and I could see with my own eyes that the *auil* controlled the best lands in our district.

Thick mat-grass covered the little-used roadway. It wafted up a damp breeze, which cooled our faces gently after a hot day. Off in the distance we saw thick rows of trees, planted in a bowed formation to protect the lands against the searing steppe winds. Every so often the road skirted a lake, and then the wind that blew at our backs was tangled and stilled in the impregnable walls of bulrushes. It seemed as though this piece of land had been created for no other purpose but to glory in the inimitable beauty of our vast steppes.

We were heading toward a rather sparse grove of birches. From afar it looked as though the trees were besieged on all sides by hordes of plant lice. As we came closer the picture proved far less mysterious: these were squat mud-houses, worn down by rain and harried by the winds.

The wintering grounds of Zhanbyrshi were completely deserted, and we continued onward. Soon we came to a lush green dale, strewn with some dozen blackened yurts. A few horses met us along the road; cows grazed in twos and threes; handfuls of sheep and goats scattered listlessly as we came near. It was impossible not to notice how emaciated the animals looked. Nothing but walking corpses, skin pulled over bones … The previous winter had been mild. I knew that all across our district herds, flocks, and folds went out to spring pastures in good health.

We entered the modest *auil*, marveling and trying to make sense of what we'd seen. Why did these animals look like they had just barely made it through a fierce *jut*?

A handful of young girls, leaning against the felt walls of the yurts, followed our progress with utter indifference. One of them, who seemed older than her mates, gave an idle yawn and rubbed a bare foot against an ankle. No boys came running—as they invariably do—to make a grab for the cart and be chased off with a brandished whip.

A group of men sat motionlessly on a low knoll at the very center of the *auil*. Coming up to them I pulled up the reins, and my gelding, exhausted by our morning excesses, halted obligingly.

It had been a warm day, but all the men sat in their *tymaks*—winter hoods that went down to cover the shoulders. Here and there tufts of fur were coming out of the *tymaks*.

The men had long noticed the arrival of a stranger's cart, but they kept their proud, sovereign silence. A few heads turned just slightly in our direction.

What could we do but ignore their disdain and make our introductions? I went up to the group and held out my hand to the nearest man.

"No, no, my good fellow!" he protested and shoved his hands even deeper into the sleeves of his tattered coat. "Not me … First you must greet the *aqsaqal*." And he nodded toward an old man, whose sunken mouth moved up and down without making the least sound. It seemed as though his words were caught in his half-gray, half-red beard no sooner than they escaped his lips.

"As-salaum 'agaleikum." I turned to him.

The old man raised his head in a manner that made evident his great sense of self-worth.

"Uagaleikum ash'shalam!"

After this he fell back into silence. It seemed he hadn't noticed that his lordly mien did not accord with his toothless "ash'shalam," or the leaky yurts that stood round us, or the wasted cattle we had met along the road.

But we had to continue our introductions. I turned to my left and let my hand dangle in mid-air.

"Now you must greet the man who sits at the right hand of our esteemed Ateke …"

Surmising that Ateke was the red-bearded elder, I gave my hand to his equally bearded but moustacheless neighbor. He returned my greeting in a mullah's sonorous voice, used to calling out prayers:

"Ua-ga-lei-kum, as-sa-lam!"

I was about to proceed down the line in the same direction, but was once again corrected.

"This way, this way," protested the master of ceremonies. "Now you must give greeting to the man who sits at the left hand of Ateke …"

I crisscrossed their circle, following a strict hierarchy. In the time it took me to perform this ceremony, the whole *auil* could have packed up and set off for the next pasture.

Finally all the hands were duly shaken, and Ateke mumbled:

"Korash, you make room … This place would be most appropriate for our young guest."

Korash made a sour face, but did not dare disobey his chief. He moved just enough for me to squeeze in beside him.

O mighty Allah! What a comic and sad spectacle they were—these men, stuffed with their pride, who could not permit themselves or anybody else to sit however they pleased. Neither before nor since had I met with such fanatical—and incongruous—adherence to protocol.

"May your comings and goings be joyful, young man—yours and those of your worthy companions." So the *aqsaqal* addressed me.

"May your wishes be granted." I bowed my head in deference and pressed my hand to my heart. "We've come here, to your village …"

But Ateke cut me short.

"For now your saying 'May your wishes be granted' is sufficient. The rest you will tell us in good time."

There was nothing to do but to lower my head and once more press my open hand to my heart.

Ateke shifted his legs and started in on the questions, indispensable to any encounter in the steppes.

"Now tell us, what is your people and your tribe?"

"I am a Kerey."

"From which Kereys?"

"From Kyzyl-Zhar[1], Ateke."

"And is it well with your people? Are you in need of anything?"

"When we left everything was well."

"Praise be to Allah, the Beneficent, the Merciful," he made up for me. "And where did you set out from this morning?"

"From Borovoe."

"Ah yes, Burabai," he corrected me. "And where does your journey end?"

"It ends right here, Ateke."

The old man's gaze traveled patiently over all present, without skipping a single man. His eyes held council with his lieutenants, and evidently they were all in agreement.

"Yesengeldy!" He turned to the man whom I had mistakenly greeted first. "Take our guests to the great yurt reserved for guests of honor. These men belong there."

The man without a moustache, who sat at Ateke's right hand, seconded the motion.

"Our Ateke has spoken well. If they have come expressly to see us, their place can only be in the great yurt."

But even after he had spoken, Yesengeldy remained seated. Evidently protocol demanded another endorsement.

My guess was momentarily confirmed.

---

1   Kyzyl-Zhar—the Kazakh name for the city of Petropavlovsk.

"Our Ateke is right. Take the travelers to the great yurt. That is where they belong."

This time the old man's injunction was echoed by a grim-looking, thickly bearded man, whose eyes were set so far apart, they seemed to be staring out of his temples. Having uttered his words he sat as still as a statue.

Nevertheless, three was evidently the magic number, because Yesengeldy sprung to his feat and announced solemnly:

"Young friends! Come, I shall take you to the great yurt, where we entertain our guests of honor."

The three of us went after him. My young friends could barely stifle their laughter, but I had the worst of it: even a hint of a smile from me would have sent them rollicking, and our whole mission would be ruined.

To keep us all in check I launched into a serious discussion with our guide.

"Yeseke, it's still early. We would have liked to address the council about the business that brought us here, to Zhanbyrshi. Tell me, when do you think we might get a chance to do that?"

"Everything has its time and place," he replied. "Here in Zhanbyrshi, Ateke himself will see about your business. When he asks you, 'What is your business here?'—that's when you tell him."

There was nothing to be done but to submit to the inviolable protocol and follow Yesengeldy. He went before us with a look on his face like he was some sultan's minister, at the very least! Like the rest of his kinsmen he seemed not to notice how ill-suited he was for that role. The wind threatened to dislodge the clumps of camel fur that hung from his hat, and the black yurt, for which we were headed, was covered with tattered felt.

Yesengeldy would have liked to make a grand gesture of throwing open the door for us, but it was hung on a single worn-down hinge and went unwillingly, kicking up dirt and screeching miserably all the while.

"Welcome!" said Yesengeldy, and fixed on me his unblinking eyes.

What I saw inside was a commingling of former affluence and abject poverty. To begin with, the whole yurt was shot through with light. Even among the poorest of shepherds I had never seen anything like it: their wives would have long laid patches on all these gaping wounds.

Five or six of the *uiks*[2]—as thick as a man's hand—still bore traces of masterful carving. The rest were improvised: some thick, others thin as reeds, and a few were not bowed, but stood like spokes inside the dome.

A wooden bed with a strangely convolute backboard was covered with a blanket patched together from scraps, and over it lay a heap of rags.

---

2   Uiks—bowed beams that support the crown of the yurt, joining it to the latticed walls.

With a magisterial gesture, Yesengledy beckoned us to take the seats of honor. A few poorly tanned goat and calf hides convulsed at the center of the yurt; there was also a horse's hide—so small it must have come from a foal.

"You can rest here," concluded our guide, and went out.

The three of us, unable to contain ourselves any longer, rolled on the floor with bulging eyes and our hands clamped over our mouths to stifle laughter. Tears poured from our eyes, and our stomach muscles were starting to ache, but we just couldn't stop laughing.

When the laughing fit had passed, my boys went out to relieve our newly-tamed gelding of his harness, and I went back to examining the contents of the yurt.

My first impression was confirmed: at some point assured prosperity had given way here to rank poverty. Just to the right of the doorway an ancient iron-clad chest stood on a low platform. Beside it stood a *kebezhe*—a large chest for keeping tableware and other household things. The *kebezhe* was equally ancient, with traces of bone inlay.

I couldn't resist peeking inside—the chest was empty.

A saddle hung from the latticed wall. Its front pommel, finished in black lacquer with silver streaks, was shaped like a duck's head. At one time that saddle cost a lot of money. But now … if anyone had gotten it into his head to tighten the saddle-strap or put his feet in the massive stirrups, its rotten leather would have crumbled to dust.

My students came back, carrying our things. Over the coarse hides we laid a thick blanket, which we had taken from one of the dormitory rooms.

"Fine … Are we going to just sit here like this, all alone? Doesn't anyone live here?" asked one of the boys.

"Sure," said the other. "There he is now!"

A shaggy dog had stuck his head through one of the larger holes and, paying little attention to the new masters, was making ready to come in. "Get out!" I said, chasing him off.

The boys and I agreed to keep our conversation to a minimum and especially to refrain from making any comments on the bewildering state of affairs that we witnessed. This was the only way we were going to find out what was really happening in Zhanbyrshi.

Outside, we heard Yesengeldy call out:

"Karashash! Hey, Karashash! We've got guests in the great yurt today. You hear? Ateke says you must go and look after them!"

"What sort of guests? Where'd they come from?" a woman's husky voice came in reply.

We looked at one another in apprehension. What have they got in store for us now? But there was nothing to be done—we sat and waited.

We heard footsteps approaching outside; the door screeched open—but it was only Yesengeldy coming back.

"In this *auil*, where your journey has brought you, it is not customary for guests to unhitch their horses. That is a host's concern."

"Thank you. Please don't be concerned," I said in an obliging voice, trying to keep to their ways. "We're young people, as you can see yourself, and we'll look after our gelding."

But Yesengeldy was implacable:

"In this *auil*, which is called Zhanbyrshi, it is not customary for guests to unhitch and look after their own horses."

He went away, and we were about to fall into another laughing fit, when an old woman appeared in the doorway. She came in just as Yesengeldy went out.

Karashash greeted us cordially—the three of us could have easily passed for her own children.

"Glory be to Allah, I've got no complaints," she said, and quickly added, "I must be used to it … And then, you can go on complaining all you like—nothing will come of it. But whatever brings you to this graveyard?"

Evidently Karashash had no trouble saying just what she thought of the people of Zhanbyrshi and their way of living. Clearly, this was the person who could tell me everything I needed to know, and for which we had set out on this journey.

I didn't even have to ask: the old woman's resentment had been brewing for a long time, and she needed to get it out.

"I don't know what you've heard," she began. "Since the ancient times there were *tore*[3] living in Zhanbyrshi … This is their land. But they wouldn't think to lift a finger in its direction. Their lot and fortune are in god's hands, as far as they are concerned! Not so long ago there were *tolengits* living among them. Thirty families in all. They did everything. But since the new times, they have all left. They're living elsewhere now, in a *kolkhoz* … Yesterday I went to gather up our cows, and I saw: their fields are plowed; they've started sowing. What's the matter with that? And look what's happening here!" She shook her head in resignation. "There is not one man in ten who'll saddle his own horse, let alone chop up some firewood or cut some hay for the winter. No, they wouldn't lift a finger to slaughter a mangy sheep. Even if their bellies were tied in knots from hunger. I do everything. I'm a *tolengit*'s daughter. I stayed back here, with these living corpses."

In the course of her story Karshash had gone out of the yurt a few times— she had put on a samovar—and quickly came back. I had heard of the *tore* of Zhanbyrshi before, but I couldn't imagine what was happening to them now.

---

3   Tore—a noble line, descending from the Mongols; they held a privileged position in the steppes. Tolengits—who could be of any lineage—lived among the tore as servants.

Most of the land around these parts belonged to them. But there wasn't a single stake in the ground that they had driven with their own hands. No, it wouldn't do their excellencies to toil. The *tolengits* had to take care of all that. They grazed the animals, cut the hay, sowed wheat and oats. They saddled the horses whenever one of the masters wished to go hunting, or riding, or anything else. The tattered *kiyiz* was all that was left of their former glory and prosperity. That, and their hereditary pride.

Karshash came back with a steaming samovar.

"Water's ready," she said, looking away, "but there's not much to go with it. I'll find some milk, that's for sure. But there's not a twig of tea in the whole *auil*, believe me ..."

We had brought our own tea—which delighted Karashash, and she set off in search of a teapot.

What she finally brought back was of a piece with the tattered *kiyiz* and the crumbling saddle: a web of black cracks stretched over the porcelain, so that it had to be held together with strips of soldered tin, while a piece of metal tubing had replaced a broken spout. There was also a set of *keses* of every size and pattern—evidently collected piecemeal from the villagers.

Karashash spread out a tablecloth, patched and darned all over, and we threw our towel over it. Luckily we had brought our own bread, butter, and sugar.

Just as we were sitting down to our supper, or snack, as it were, a group of men came into the yurt. They went in a single file, according to rank and seniority. First came Ateke. He paused beside me, his proud head raised high, and by the look on his face I knew that I had once again taken the wrong seat.

I quickly rose to make room, but the old man stopped me with a wave of his scanty beard:

"No need to go too far ... The eldest of the guests sits at my right hand."

I stayed put. My boys, on the other hand, were shuffled off to the outer edge, away from the bread and butter.

Lack of teeth didn't seem to trouble Ateke: he broke off small pieces of bread and shoved them down his gulley with astonishing speed, his whole body quivering in a single swallowing motion. The rest of the *aqsaqal* weren't about to fall behind.

The three of us had a *kese* of tea apiece, and soon there wasn't a crumb left on the table. When all was finished Ateke broke the silence:

"I must say, the butter was fresh ... Good for eating."

One after another his retinue repeated the very same words, as though not one of them had an original thought in his head, and they needed their chief to tell them what's what.

"Ateke spoke well," rejoined the moustache-less man, who sat beside me, on the other side from Ateke. "The butter was fresh. Good for eating."

I thought: "My students and I are the only ones who didn't get to test that particular theory." And I wondered what might come next, when I noticed that a few lonely nuggets of sugar had made their way onto the table.

"Shame on any man who takes his fill with no care for his children and grandchildren, flesh of his flesh," said Ateke. "Here's a treat for my little one …" His knotty black fingers gathered up three or four nuggets off the tablecloth and shoved them into his pocket.

"Ateke is always right," agreed the moustache-less man and also put out his hand. "Shame on any man who takes his fill without a thought for his children and grandchildren, flesh of his flesh."

Yesengeldy, Karash, the man with eyes in his temples, and all the rest followed their example.

There was nothing left on the table. Balancing their *keses* on fingertips, the *tore* sipped their empty tea. Only Karashash, who had found a place by the samovar, seemed put out by the sorry welcome her guests had received.

I tried several times to go out and check on my horse, but each time I was held back by the scholar and guardian of old customs. Yesengeldy insisted that in their *auil* it fell to the host to take care of the horses. There was no help for it: I had to go back to my seat while my horse was left hitched up and hungry, just as we were. Nothing could get going until Ateke formally questioned me about the purpose of our journey, but he sat silently, listening to the gurgling in his belly.

Karshash lit a lamp. It had no glass, and the wick was smoking without giving off much light. Every now and then a gust of wind came through one of the many holes in the wall and nearly put out the flame. But it sprang up again and again, casting anxious glimmers on the faces of our hosts.

Yes, one could easily take them for corpses. Nobody uttered a word and the yurt was sunk in grave silence. An eerie feeling crept over me, as though I had found myself inside a ghost tale.

But presently Ateke raised his head and cleared his throat.

"Time is passing," he said. "One would do well to slaughter a lamb for our good guests."

"Wise Ateke, the faithful guardian of ancient laws, passed down to us by our glorious ancestors, is right, as usual," rejoined the moustache-less man. "One would do well to slaughter a lamb for our illustrious guests."

The same notion was echoed by the man with broadly set eyes, whose words seemed like a call to action.

I tried to protest—there was no need for such extravagances … But nobody thought to take note of my feeble protest. I fell silent, reasoning that it wouldn't be so bad to have something of substance for a change. That morning, rushing to get underway, we had barely had breakfast.

But there was no special hurry about our supper. The men fell silent once more, savoring their extraordinary largesse. Their bellies were stuffed with pride.

The guests had little choice but to suffer in silence and reverence, but Karshash had clearly reached a boiling point.

"If it's decided, then what are they waiting for?" she said, addressing no one in particular. "If it's all discussed and decided, why are they sitting there like their backsides are rooted to the earth? O Allah! Allah, the All-merciful! Do you see? Will you ever rid us of these cursed ways? These are living people sitting here, not some corpses!"

She sprung to her feet and went out of the yurt. The shaggy mutt, who had found his way into the yurt, and whose prospects of getting a scrap had grown dim, ran after her.

But the woman's outburst did little to shake the men's composure. Ateke waited a while longer before announcing his decision.

"There is sense in what Karashash says, although she has spoken rashly. Time is passing … Since it's been discussed and decided, it must be done."

His two lieutenants followed suit, like echoes rolling in the mountains. But not a man budged from his seat.

Karshash knew what she had to do: she brought in a heap of firewood and threw it down beside the hearth. She came back a second time with a blackened cauldron, and a third—with a tripod. All the while she never stopped prodding her masters into action.

"What are we waiting for? Whose sheep should we take? We still have to bring it here," she entreated them, but as soon as she was outside we could hear her complaints and curses.

Choosing the proper sheep proved no easy matter.

"Yesengeldy!" commanded Ateke. "Why don't you speak up? Your grandmother has a sheep, a gray one … It seems to me this gray sheep is the one for our cauldron."

The same sentiment was echoed on either side of the chief, after which Yesengeldy rose silently and went out. Silence reigned in the yurt once more. From outside I could hear the plaintive neighing of my black, who had long despaired of seeing a scrap of hay, let alone a bag of oats.

Yesengeldy came back. He lowered himself onto his knees and only then addressed Ateke.

"Aisha-*kelin*[4] says: the gray sheep will calve any day now … It would be a sin to slaughter the animal at such time."

"Aisha-*kelin* knows," confirmed Ateke. "That would be a sin, indeed. Any day now the gray sheep will calve."

---

4 Kelin—a young married woman.

But the keepers of ancient customs were evidently somewhat enlivened by the prospect of tasting fresh meat. For this reason, perhaps, Ateke kept his deliberations shorter than usual.

"Here is what we'll do: bring us the black lamb from Kanshi-*zhengei*'s[5] house. It is one of our newest lambs, and is well fit for slaughter."

Yesengeldy was equally anxious, and he got up even before the moustache and the temples could make their customary rejoinders, and by the time they finished he was long gone. But soon he was back.

His excursion had met with failure once again. Yesengeldy said bleakly:

"Aizhan-*kelin* met me on the way … She says: this Friday it will be two years since Kanshi-*zhengei*'s death. Aizhan is saving the lamb, that she might have a little something with which to commemorate that good woman."

"Right, right," said Ateke, clearly disappointed. "Aizhan is right …"

He fell to thinking once more, but his empty stomach, which had barely taken notice of our bread and butter, had obviously quickened his wandering mind. Ateke promptly came up with another eligible victim.

"Enough empty talk!" he said firmly. "Talk is not going to fill our cauldron! Yesengeldy, bring us the gray goat that belongs to Kareke."

It was past midnight when we heard the shrill protests of the stubborn goat. But Yesengeldy was full of determination—our supper was entering the realms of probability.

The goat, which we couldn't see, announced its presence with a thick, heavy stench. This was a breeder goat, ungelded. A mere mortal might have easily suffocated, which is what nearly happened to me. But not to the Khan's illustrious progeny. Their nostrils were obviously made of different stuff. They paid no attention to the smell, reasoning, perhaps, that cooking would get rid of it. Their eyes sparkled; their palettes salivated. Each man could have devoured a whole goat, dead or living, down to the meanest scrap.

But there was another obstacle. Nobody had a sufficiently sharp knife for the job. Ateke remembered very well which house had a good knife, but his emissary, Yesengeldy, returned empty-handed.

One of my comrades-in-sorrow, exasperated by the long, tedious wait, the hunger, and the stench, jumped to his feet and held out his knife to Yesengeldy.

"Please take this," he said, though I could see in his eyes that he would have just as soon sent all of these men to *shaitan*, and left Zhanbyrshi, never to return again.

It was dawning when the old goat came back, dished out in an old washtub. The tub was attended by some dozen women, and each woman was leading a child by the hand.

---

5   Zhengei—an old woman.

There were maybe two boys among them—the rest were girls. The children had been woken up; they were yawning and rubbing their eyes. All of them looked sickly. The ancient law that reigned in Zhanbyrshi demanded strict purity of the illustrious bloodline, and for this reason most of the marriages involved close relatives. The children were a sorry sight.

The women greedily inhaled the emanations rising from the washtub. But a goat is certainly no bull … There was hardly enough to feed such a crowd.

By right, Ateke took up the goat's head, cut off an ear, and handed it to me. The head stayed with him. The moustache extracted the pelvic bone, sliced off a modest chunk—again, for me—and laid the rest at his knees. Everyone grabbed whatever piece they were entitled to, according to their rank. Chunks of meat were flying off the bones here and there, but not a single one reached the tub. Snatched up in mid-air by deft hands they vanished, never to be heard from again.

The meal did not last very long. Our hosts gulped down the *sorpa* after the meat, distributed the neatly picked bones among the children, wished us a good night, and dispersed.

All at once, the yurt was empty.

We talked a while longer with Karashash. The good woman was worried that her guests would go to sleep hungry.

But we had no mind to sleep. Not waiting until Ateke could find a propitious moment to question us, and breaking the custom according to which guests in Zhanbyrshi can never take care of their own horses, we went out to harness my dark gelding.

We didn't just leave. We ran. We ran from these people, who had turned their *auil* into a living graveyard, ran from their arrogance and stupidity into the freedom of the open steppes.

"You'd have to wait a lifetime for a single word of substance from these people!" exclaimed one of the boys.

"And another lifetime," rejoined the other, "until this word—spoken with utter solemnity, of course—turned into action."

I listened to them in silence. I was appalled by the injustice of history. How many centuries, how many fruitless centuries had we lost—we, the Kazakh people—while these *tore* ruled over us?

… The following morning I made my report to the district secretary—it was short and to the point.

"The *auil* of Zhanbyrshi controls enough land to accommodate four *kolkhozes*. But there is only one person among the villagers who could be of any use in a *kolkhoz*. This person is a woman called Karashash, a *tolengit's* daughter."

"Is that so? And what are we going to do with the rest of them?"

I was young then, and quick on the draw. I repeated:

"There is only one person in the whole *auil*, that could be of any use in a *kolkhoz* ..."

The district secretary was silent.

1956

Ballad of Years Long Past

(*excerpt*)

By Abish Kekilbaev

That devastating raid was Zhoneut's last campaign. Zhoneut came back with six captive youths, six maids, and a troubled mind.

The once glorious bloodline has been sapped—no true *batyr* are left to it. All have withered and died out. Meanwhile, old age has crept up on Zhoneut. All that is left now is but idle talk of former glory.

There is no one to succeed him, no one to take his place at the head of the tribe.

His eldest son was strong and stout, like a saxaul. He had no equal when it came to the dagger, the sword, or the spear. His sharp eye never failed him— there was no one who could rival him in marksmanship. He was very young when he saw his first campaign, and he was still young when he saw his last. There is his grave, just outside the *auil*.

The middle son was a brawler and a bully. As soon as he was able to stand on his own two legs he was already swinging his fists. Everyone had gotten a taste of those fists—his playmates and his dogs. A hard-headed and short-tempered man, he felt no pity for man or animal. Nothing pleased his ear more than news of a quarrel or brawl. He idolized the brazen warrior Kök-boré, and clung to him like a puppy. He met his end far from his native land. At least there was a grave somewhere …

The youngest, Daulet, grew up tall and broad-shouldered. "He'll take a *jigit* on each arm," men joked. He had never been pinned to the ground at any of the festival contests.

Daulet is handsome—with large, clear eyes, a high and smooth forehead, and a bright face, unusual for a Turkmen. A pair of bushy eyebrows lend his face a stern expression, but his radiant eyes speak of an inner softness.

Daulet is everyone's darling. Even fearsome hounds—Allah forbid the reader run across their paths—seeing him, wag their tails and fawn for his favor with a friendly whine.

Rumors have reached Zhoneut that his son has met with success among the young maidens of the village. No harm in that, thinks Zhoneut. Only once did he reproach his son, when Daulet brought to his *yurt* the widow of a warrior fallen in battle. The memory of a *batyr* is sacred.

Everyone in the family loved Daulet, except his uncle Kök-boré. Kök-boré was a fierce and fearless man, and he valued only these qualities in others. Nothing else mattered to him. It made him angry to hear that Daulet was engaging in activities not worthy of a *jigit*. Kök-boré had little doubt about what was and what was not a man's pursuit. A horseman must be an expert at arms. If he isn't, then he is no horseman. Let him look after sheep.

Daulet listened to these speeches with a good-natured smile and had no thought of changing his ways. His passion had manifested itself early on in his childhood—it was music. The *baksi* and the *dutar* player are dearer to Daulet than his own flesh and blood, and the song sounds sweeter than the chime of clashing daggers. Since his fifteenth year he has not parted with his *dutar*, and he has attained such mastery that Yahia himself, the famed musician from Tachauz, listened to his playing with tears streaming down his cheeks.

The days of Zhoneut are filled with campaigning, and his nights are seldom spent in bed. Music, song, merrymaking—all that is the *djinns'* sabbath, as far as he is concerned. On this point Zhoneut is in agreement with his brother Kök-boré.

Daulet knows his father's heart, and he would not dare take down the *dutar* in his presence.

But Daulet also has a protector: his other uncle Annadurdy is a lover and connoisseur of arts. Once, on a mission to the Aday, Annadurdy brought his nephew along, and there he tasted glory. In a contest he bested many famed musicians, and he shared the first prize with a young Kazakh *kuyshi*.

Zhoneut didn't say a word then, but inside he was pleased—his son had been victorious. Kök-boré, on the other hand, was outraged: "That's just what we need in this family!" For him, a triumph among musicians—"a shameless horde of criers and idlers"—was an outright disgrace.

Kök-boré showered his brother with angry reproaches, refused to sit in the seat of honor, and spent the entire evening cursing and lamenting.

"Your son is a *dutar*-player!" he shouted at Zhoneut, until his wizened throat grew purple from the strain. "A *dutar*-player! Only evil could ever come from this! The enemy fears a warrior on horseback, not an imbecile with a *dutar* in his hands … In the old days the sight of any one of our men could drive fear into the hearts of the Aday, and today we tickle their ears with our music!" He let out of pitiful squeal, mocking Daulet. "They should be running the moment they lay eyes upon us," the *batyr* went on, "and they won't be running from our songs! Daulet's soul has become the refuge of *djinns*. They have made him forget about honor and vengeance. When I think that for a full month he lived among our enemies and feasted with them, as though he had come among his own kin … How could I ever live down such disgrace? The most wretched of our women never sank this low.

Look at him"—Kök-boré stuck out his finger at his nephew—"he's even proud of himself! His heart is glad, as though he is a warrior returning from a victorious raid. And Annadurdy is glad too. 'When Daulet played his *dutar*, even our mortal enemies clicked their tongues in approval.' O empty-headed vanity, stoked by an enemy's praise! If your enemy praises you, you may be sure he is scheming against you. If you're not smart enough to see that, then you'd better stay home, crouching over a goat's hide and telling fortunes with *dzhida*-berries … If a real *jigit* had paid a visit to the Aday in place of Daulet, they would not be making merry, they would not be clicking their tongues from pleasure—they would have swallowed their tongues from fright! Songsters, *dutar*-players, *baksi*—these aren't men, they're vermin; they're women who swoon when they see men coming. A *batyr*'s might is in his spear and dagger, not his song and *dutar*. What use is song when it comes to defending your people?

"This pansy Daulet laughs at my words: 'Why don't you cool off a little, uncle,' he tells me. 'You think we're better off fighting the Aday, carrying off their wives and horses? You're angry when you hear that innocent Kazakhs haven't been slaughtered, that their herds are grazing peacefully in the steppes?' Those are his own vile words!

"I remind him of our ancestors' honor, of the spirit of vengeance—and all he can do is laugh. 'Let our ancestors lie in peace,' he says. 'They've spilled plenty of blood in their time, and they ended up spilling their own. Maybe there is a lesson in that …' So now our ancestors' blood means nothing to this wag …"

Kök-boré raged all night long. To appease him, Zhoneut promised to speak to his son, who had by then gone out to rejoin the revelers. As they parted, Zhoneut told his brother:

"Don't be angry. He's still a boy. He'll wise up in time."

Those were not the words that Kök-boré wished to hear. From that day on he never set foot in his brother's *yurt*.

Meanwhile, Daulet continued his carefree life, full of music and revelry. Until the death of Kök-boré, Zhoneut turned a blind eye and never reproached his son.

After the funeral, when they had eaten the white colt over Kök-boré's grave and put to torture the six captive Kazakh youths, Zhoneut summoned his son.

They were left alone with the night. Her shooting stars cut across the heavens over them and her crickets chirped everywhere about them. And her captives moaned and howled and gnashed their teeth from the miserable hovel, where they were kept.

Daulet was silent. His sensitive ear took in the pitiful cries and the clangor of chains. But he did not hear the snores and the sighs that rose up from the neighboring *yurts*, nor did he imagine that the *auil* could sleep on such a night.

Daulet sat crouching before his father, and seemed to him almost a small child. And Zhoneut felt his heart brimming over with love and tenderness for his young son.

The night wind streamed in through the low opening of the yurt and cooled Zhoneut's throbbing temples. He too listened to the sounds of the sleeping *auil*, and he heard the moaning and the chains that had troubled his son. He pictured the captives rolling on the ground, and in desperation bringing the shackles down on their own heads.

Could it be that Daulet was moved to pity by the miserable lot of these prisoners, and not by his uncle's death? Has he really turned into a faint-hearted, sniveling child?

Zhoneut noticed his son's shoulders trembling slightly. He remembered that as they stood beside Kök-boré's grave, his son had not shed a single tear. His face was as pale and stiff as a linen shroud. But now the suffering of the filthy Aday have impressed him more than the death of his warrior uncle!

O, Kök-boré was a thousand times right. The cursed *dutar*, those cursed songs have driven all sense of honor from his son's heart. He has forgotten about his ancestors' honor, about sacred vengeance. If a man can no longer make his enemy pay blood for blood, then he has no business wearing a sheepskin *papakha*. He might as well be gelded. Then he can weep over the wretched cries of those degenerates all day long …

Still, Zhoneut did not utter a single word. He pulled the striped quilt over his head and went to sleep.

When he woke up, Daulet was gone.

"Bring him!"

His son returned, looking haggard and downcast. His eyes appeared glazed, his cheeks sunken. Silently, he poured out his father's tea from a brightly painted *kuman*, and sat down before him.

Zhoneut followed his son's movements with a pained expression. But once more he could not bring himself to speak.

A few more days passed. Zhoneut was getting ready for a hunting expedition, and for the first time he asked his son to accompany him. Their horses galloped through the steppe, pursued by two lean and ruddy hounds.

Zhoneut needed to be alone with his son. The angry words of Kök-boré would not let him rest. How prescient they seemed now! Kök-boré had seen into Daulet's heart, made soft by music. Perhaps he could not grasp the whole of Daulet's nature, but he saw the problem as clear as day.

like a dark blade. A heap of stones had been piled up at the tip, and a pillar placed beside it—a marker of a holy man's final rest.

This was the grave of Temir-baba. The two men came down from their saddles and approached on foot, leading the horses by their bridles. They came to a large stone with a charred depression at its center. This is where pilgrims lit their sacred fires.

From a long exposure to the sun the grave marker had grown black, and the wind had made it smooth and shiny. The rags tied to the pillar fluttered in the sea breeze.

There were bones, skulls, and horns of urial among the boulders ... Many pilgrims had spent the night beside this holy grave.

Without uttering a single word, Zhoneut knelt and recited a prayer. He raised his hands to the heavens, then he passed his palms over his forehead, his eyes, his cheeks, his beard. Still muttering, he got up to his feet, tore the rags from the pillar, and stuffed them into his shirt.

The two men went on, all the while leading the horses by hand. At the top of the mound the wind whipped the horses' manes and clapped the skirts of their *shapans*.

Once, many centuries ago, Shopan-ata was returning from Khoresm and he met Temir-baba in this place. Temir-baba sat on a stone and bathed his tired feet in the gently lapping waters. He heard footsteps approaching from a distance, but he never turned his head. The traveler approached and greeted him courteously, but Temir-baba never took his eyes off the sea.

Shopan-ata named himself, inquired after the other man's name, and proposed a contest.

"Very well," said Temir-baba, "if you like, you may go first."

"So be it," agreed Shopan-ata. "In that case, please be kind enough to turn around. Do you see that pack of *karakuiruk*?"

"I do."

Then Shopan-ata called in a barely audible whisper:

"*Shore-shore-shore.*"

The leader of the pack pricked up his ears and, obedient to the call, ran bleating to Shopan-ata, stretched out at his feet, and licked the skirt of his *shapan*.

But that was not the end of the marvel. Without a knife, Shopan-ata slit the goat's throat, stripped off its hide in the blink of an eye, cut open its belly, and divided up the flesh. Then he wrapped the pieces in the hide and passed his hand over it. All at once the goat sprang to its feet, shook the dust from its sides, and raced back to rejoin the pack.

Then it was Temir-baba's turn. He rolled his pants up to his knee and waded into the foaming sea waters. He walked on and on, never pausing for a moment, and the sea obediently spread open before him. Wherever he set down his foot, the ground rose up to meet it. He walked for a long time, until at last

That was how the old *batyr*, Zhoneut's grandfather, saw things. But his ideas did not always agree with the way things were in real life. Neither the sands nor deserts stood in the way of the enemy when he set his heart on another man's goods and his cattle. The enemy cares nothing for the sacred memory of your ancestors, for the pride and pain of your people!

The greedy enemy first puts out his hand to take your animals, and once he has eaten his fill he dreams of making himself the master of your steppe, of taking his pleasure with your daughters.

O simple-hearted people, you that read the weather by the steed's belly and your troubles by the dogs' howl. Do you see the danger that rides forth to meet you? Do you know that the enemy may come in secret, his rope hidden in his wide sleeve—and by the time he has twisted the noose about your neck and thrown you down at his feet, it is already much too late?

———————————

The scorching noon-hour is passed. Slowly a hint of blue creeps back into the blazing sky. Against it stands the sharp silhouette of the lone watchman, like a grave pillar marking a *korgan*.

Zhoneut turned his gaze from the watchman and peered into the faces of the *aksakal*. The elders shifted uneasily under his gaze. They sensed trouble—the expedition should have retuned long ago. But before any one of them could open his mouth, they saw a shudder run through the figure of the gaunt watch-man, and a wave passed over the hairs on his *shapan*. Everyone started.

Somewhere in the west, beyond the edges of the *auil*, a long cry shot up into the heavens. Zhoneut shut his eyes, as though from a brilliant flash. The strength drained from his legs. He made an awkward lunge before he could finally get up. By then the *yurt* was empty, and he was the last to come out.

By custom, a watchman announces the return of a victorious expedition. With the joyous cry "Suinshi! Suinshi!" he races toward the *auil*.

Zhoneut tried to concentrate. What direction are the *jigit* coming from? Why hadn't the watchman seen them? Why has the auspicious cry "Suinshi!" given way to a heart-wrenching wail?

The questions seemed to multiply without end. Who are the people riding this way, so heavy in their saddles? Where is the dappled steed? Why is a white rag tied to the spear of the leading horseman?

The *jigit* came closer. The dust over their heads grew thicker, blocking out the sun. Their mournful "Wo-o-oe!" has already reached the *auil*, and a groan rose up from within the village in answer.

The horsemen swayed in their saddles, clung to their horses' manes, and seemed stooped beneath their wooly *papakhas*.

black *kiyiz*. The procession headed toward a hillock. It seemed as though the entire village had come out to follow them.

He too went along, blindly, understanding nothing of what was happening. His legs felt weak, as though he had been walking like this for many days, perhaps many months. He should have been at the head of the procession, but there he was, shuffling along with the frail old men at the tail.

Other young men have come forward to help carry the long object draped in black. It must be heavy. Now they are lowering it to the ground with great care.

The mullah has started up again. Heeding his words, men race toward the brushwood, encircling the cemetery. Yes, it is the cemetery ... They draw their swords and strike at the brush, again and again. Why are they in such a hurry? Now a great pit lies open before them—where has it come from? And the heap of dry branches ...?

A young *jigit* has returned his sword to its sheath and taken a flint stone from his pocket. A flame has engulfed the branches, casting a scarlet glare over faces, stilled by prayer. In the evening hush one could make out so sharply every last crackle of the flames, and the muffled syllables of the mullah's prayer.

The black *kiyiz* is unfurled. What lay inside it is lowered into the great pit. But why are they moving so quickly? Why not wait a little longer?

It all seems like a dream. Of course, it is a dream. You can make out certain movements, but their meaning is uncertain. That is why your soul is filled with strange foreboding. You must will yourself to wake up. This is just what Zhoneut is about to do. Then all this mournful agitation will scatter and peace will take its rightful place.

But the thrice-cursed dream will not let up.

Someone has gotten hold of a few shovels, and now they are tossing clods of earth into the pit. The black emptiness of the pit has turned into a ruddy heap of earth. Mambetpana—was he here all along?—has thrust a shovel into his hands, and now he is guiding his arms in a shoveling motion ...

A stupor has come over Zhoneut and will not let him be. The world is spinning before his eyes.

But he is not a weak man. He will shake off this confusion.

Once more, they are leading him by the arms, and his legs are slowly regaining their strength.

But all the commotion will not let him gather his thoughts; it pulls him back into the interrupted dream.

A new bout of frenzy has seized the crowd. What is happening? An enemy attack? Then where are the horses? Can it be that he, *batyr* Zhoneut, has slept through an enemy incursion? What's happened to the women and children? Why, why is he nowhere to be seen—their joy and comfort, their Daulet? Why did the youngest son leave his father's side?

The Old and the Young

By Didar Amantay

Years ago, in the haymaking months, me and my grandfather Toleutai often rode down to the foot of pine-covered Tonkeris, which abuts the Karakaly range. In the early morning our old araba with wooden wheels made its lumbering progress along the meandering country road. Rising before dawn and making a dreadful racket on the cobblestone street, we hurried to make our way out of the desolate *auil*, sunk in its peaceful slumber. The entire journey grandpa sat stock still at the reins, never making the slightest movement. I let my feet dangle off the back of the cart and surveyed the fleeting road in a dreamy half-daze. Sometimes a song would come into my mind, though I could never remember any of its words. I just made up something to go along with the melody and sang it quietly to myself.

Later I moved to a bustling city, full of noise and chaos. Nearly every evening I would get a call from Marat, and the two of us set out on our nightly peregrinations, coming home long past midnight, worn out by our wanderings and conversation. Usually we ended up at the café Zhuldyz and stayed there late into the night, nursing our drinks, until there was no one but the two of us left in the whole place. Marat would pour out the cognac, push the glasses out into the center of the table, and announce quietly:

"Here's to good health."

I nodded in agreement. Dusk had been gathering steadily about the brown-colored walls of the interior, and we found our troubled souls sunk beneath the weight of a melancholy that rose up within us. Attending each to his own gloomy thoughts, and careful not to disturb the other, we slowly drifted away from the *dastarkhan* that lay between us. At times, the great effort to preserve the ceremonial silence or to plumb the depths of various phenomena left me with a terrible headache. At such times I understood the world to be full of lies. I wanted to explain my latest findings to Marat, but he understood me without a single word. Deftly refilling our glasses, he gazed at me impassively for a long time, until a smile came gradually to the surface of his still face. Then Marat would say:

"Aidar, all is emptiness in this life."

I never tried to argue or persuade him otherwise. I only smiled politely in answer to his strained, frozen smile. Everything seemed to me a lie. And yet precisely at such moments our spirits would be lifted. We never derived any pleasure or self-satisfaction from spotting errors or weaknesses in one another's arguments. For some unknown reason a soft, warm feeling ran like a current through our nervous systems, penetrating even into the analytical part of the brain.

"Here is to friendship," Marat would say.

"No," I protested, "instead let us swear that there'll be no more lying from this moment forward. To that."

"To that," he agreed.

"Today there is no truth for men to worship. And this is why you'll find but a handful of true friends in this world, friends that could never betray you."

"To truth."

"Do you know why people are so quick to betray one another?"

"No."

"Neither do I."

"But not everyone is like that."

"No, of course not everyone."

"And that is the truth."

A briefly deposed silence resumed its reign. It seemed as if that inviolate hush, launched from a distant shore at the moment when the sheer cliffs had swallowed up the roar of the sea, and wandering all through the world ever since, had stumbled upon us, seated at one of the tables at café Zhuldyz, and now held us firmly in its grasp. On such days, effaced by their very drabness, we were naturally drawn to the female sex. There were plenty of girls in the café, though most of them were quick to make their way to the dance floor, while Marat and I continued with our drinking.

Presently I would note that I divided our senseless existence, which to this day hadn't done anyone any good, precisely in half. And then this mortal life, and my generation, living in these inconstant times, the twentieth century, and our ancestors who had bestowed it upon us, and the crimes and joys of our age, and the parties and movements that prevailed in it—all of it filled me with disgust. In such moments of great internal agitation I suddenly saw with absolute clarity that there was not another soul left in all of this boundless, silent universe but me, alone—and then I cast a frightened glance at Marat.

With a gulp of his cognac, he had hooked a slice of meat with his fork, and this combination was now traveling languidly toward his listless mouth. I peered intently into his face, as though in his indifference, in his refusal to en-gage in any form of contemplation, I had discovered the key to the mystery of the universe. And at such times it all seemed a great lie. Next I would discover that I felt completely alienated from Marat, who had no thought of the world around him, but gave himself over to the pleasures of the moment. Reasoning that his actions and the eruptions of his consciousness lay outside the scope of my attention, I began to move away from him, until at last I saw that he was part of a life that was entirely alien to me and had no bearing on my own life. The great Universe was expanding right before my eyes and rising up against me with all its potentialities.

I would say, "Let's have a bit more."

"Let's."

"Are you afraid of death?"

"No."

"I am."

"Well, show me someone who isn't."

"There is no happiness in the world."

"I wouldn't go that far."

"All of us are condemned to a cruel fate."

"Man is unhappy for the simple reason that his nature demands happiness. That's what makes him so miserable."

Having apportioned the last of the bottle between us, he carefully examined its label. This was a little trick, a building up to the final toast that could lift our spirits and cheer our defenseless, melancholy hearts. At such moments everything around us seemed a great lie. Dejected, we wandered out of the café and made our way to the desolate bus stop, where we tapped one foot against the other, while the frigid cold pinched our cheeks.

Each time I went back to the *auil* I found Toleutai-*ata* grown older, more worn out, like an old piece of clothing. He was turning into a helpless old man. On my last visit in the spring he had grown so weak he couldn't get around on his own. He only recognized me after I had pulled him to myself, slid his hand into my palm, and called out my name. The old man tried to restrain his joy at seeing me, but he was soon overwhelmed by his emotions. And all I could do was to press his slight fingers to my chest, again and again.

"How good that you've come."

"Yes," I said.

"I've always had great faith in you, god bless you."

"You should sit up a bit more straight, *ata*."

"Eh, my good boy, most of the folks my age—those who had made it back from the war, that is—are already rolled in the sheet and resting in eternity."

"Do you remember how the two of us would be up before dawn, driving toward the mountains, and how you cut the grass for hours and hours, how you cut down the sweet-scented alfalfa to the very roots?"

"You were still a little boy then."

"Nowadays I wouldn't mind going a few rounds with that scythe."

"Come July, god willing, we'll find you a good harness and a horse, and an araba for such a worthy cause."

"Haven't we got them here?"

"Things tend to wander off when there's nobody to look after them."

His eyes, glazed over with white film, his body, shrunken so drastically it seemed to be no greater than the palm of my hand, the creases that had mercilessly covered his face—all of it reminded me of those enchanting years of my life, of my childhood. At every stroke grandfather laid low a sizeable swath of the thick, luxuriant stand that had grown unchecked in the gorges and ravines, about the springs and along the streams, with is tall green grass blades swaying in the pleasant breeze. He never tired. Meanwhile, I lay in the shade on a piece of pelt, mesmerized by the progress of a grasshopper that made his way up a blade of grass. Every now and then I would turn my head to look at grandpa at his work, and I would find that he had already moved some ways toward the slope of the distant mountain.

"*Ata-au*," I said, pulling his face close to mine. "You're stooping a bit too much these days."

"You were only a little boy then," he repeated.

Grandpa liked to talk to me about politics. He was only a year younger than the revolution. In 1939 he signed up for military service at the Karkaly district office and wound up in Siberia. Two years later he was headed home, when the storm broke. Grandpa came back from the war badly wounded. He had lived through mass slaughter, faced many trials and bitter losses. The few kindred spirits he managed to find among the hordes of rough soldiers were all taken from him, felled at one time or another by a German bullet. And then grandpa would curse his days and complain bitterly of having been born in such cruel times. Everyone knows that the Soviet Army had won a Great Victory in that war, but time delivers its own judgment, and in the days of the Khrushchev Thaw we learned also of the fantastic losses sustained by the victors. The Soviet generals prevailed against the far more advanced German armies because in their inexorable struggle with fascism they raised the living shield of human bodies, resulting in an unimaginable number of Soviet casualties. Grandpa didn't believe any of it. He called Stalin a brilliant strategist, and recounted tales of purges in the party ranks as though they were some hallowed legends. He exalted in the heroic deeds and selfless sacrifices of ordinary Soviet citizens, holding forth about the lofty ideals of the Socialist movement. I didn't trust any of the figures he cited, could not accept a single argument he put forth, but it

pitiful folds. I saw that any criticism of Stalin or communists hurt him deeply, so that he was likely to fall ill.

At that moment I didn't care who Stalin was, or what the Bolsheviks had done. I wanted to protect him. He resembled a small child, left all alone, who had wandered out in search of his mother and was quickly lost in unfamiliar hallways. My brother left, which made me feel better. Toleutai-*ata* turned to me. He pressed me to his chest—like in the old days—and breathed in the scent of my hair. But this time it was *I* who wanted to stand up for *him*, to shield him from harm.

"What's the weather like in Almaty?" inquired grandpa. His face had relaxed, and he wanted to turn the conversation to a different subject.

I knew that sometimes grandpa liked to start up a conversation removed as far as possible from the matters that troubled him; he wanted to chat about the trivialities of everyday life, or to ponder its swift and inexorable progress—basically to have a long and intimate conversation on some abstract topic. But he was also quick to abandon his chosen theme. What the old man really needed was a kind and solicitous word that sprang from a sympathetic heart—and he believed that I would speak the words that he longed for. Grandpa was right—I never said anything to upset him.

Sometimes, rising early in the morning, he would perch in front of the radio, to hear the latest news. One night, troubled and unable to sleep, I lay in bed thinking of all manner of things. At dawn, still awake and exhausted by my thoughts, I saw that grandpa was about to make for the radio. He lowered his feet from his bed and wrapped them in strips of fabric—and this way, unsteady but noiselessly, he made his way to the kitchen, where he kept his radio. I followed him on tip-toes through the house, and discovered that grandpa listened to the morning news, grumbling and even cursing all the while. In his last years I rarely saw him smile. The image of him that I saw that day has stayed with me all along. Leaning back in his chair, he twisted his body and stretched his neck up, toward the speaker hung on the wall. Seeing him like this, I felt slightly ill for some reason. And immediately I cringed: how could I feel disgust for my own grandfather?

The following day I returned to the city. And once more Marat and I made our useless rounds through the evening streets, ambling along the broad boulevards while strangers scurried senselessly about us. Often he tried to win me over to his outlook on women. At every opportunity he insisted that he couldn't stand women, especially when it came to women who had caught his attention, whom he loved or lusted after. Spotting a pair of black-eyed beauties on the trolley he would launch immediately into a fiery invective, pointing out all of their physical flaws and accusing them of god only knows what sins.

"Marat," I would tell him.

"Eh?"

"You like girls. Why do you go about tearing them to bits?"

This made him angry. He didn't like it that I had seen this bright glimmer in his heart—his love for women.

"Don't get mad."

"What in the world gave you that idea?"

"I could just tell."

"Well, there's nothing to it."

"I'm sorry. It's not my business. I shouldn't have said anything."

"Don't worry about it."

"I'm sorry."

"Why don't we drop in at Zhuldyz?"

Of course, there was nowhere else for us to go. I had the sensation that at some point in our lives the train of time had jumped the tracks and screeched to a dead halt.

A waiter named Saian, whom we both knew, was working that night. When Marat and I had come to Zhuldyz that final time, a rakish young man was tending the *mangal* set up just outside the café, turning the long skewers packed with sizzling meat over the hot ash and smoldering coals. Seeing us, Saian came out, we embraced and said our greetings. The *shashlyks*, neatly lined up on the grill, had browned nicely and gave off a dizzying scent that quickly roused our appetites. We passed through the main room, crowded with tables, and came out to the summer terrace. Saian led us to a table set up in the far corner and went back inside. Soon he came back, carrying a tray with a bottle of Seppelt Riesling. Embarrassed by his own choice of drink, Saian promised that later there would be good beer.

"Don't worry about us," Marat told him.

"No. Today I'll take care of you myself."

"Marat, looks like we'll be waited on by the most progressive of waiters."

"To Saian, then."

"To his good will."

"He's the best of the lot."

Saian went off again and came back with several sticks of *shashlyk*. After a toast we fell greedily on the meat, chasing it down with flat bread and wine. That night we couldn't stop telling anecdotes. We talked of politics and made sarcastic remarks about our various leaders. When thick night had fallen all around us we sensed that we had been talking too much. Then the three of us smoked in silence, blowing, from time to time, into the expiring embers of our cigarettes. At that moment everything seemed to me a great lie.

I felt an inexplicable anger swelling up within. Everything that I had done the day before was suddenly revealed to me in clear light, as though a fog that had shrouded my past days and my tomorrows suddenly cleared—the thought of having to settle, to accept this fate settled like dust over my heart and made it heavy, leaden with grief.

"Marat, you talk too much," I said all of a sudden.

"And you?"

"I do too."

"Guys, why talk this way?"

"Saian, you're a good guy. But everything around us is a lie."

"Aidar, enough of this—don't you know anything else?"

"I've stopped paying attention to you ages ago—it's just empty talk, all of it."

"And you've got some pearls of wisdom, I suppose?"

"No, but you talk too much, and it's worth noting. A puffed-up windbag is what you are. And you can't live without women."

"I despise all girls. They can swear up and down to be true, but they're always itching to betray their guy for a moment's pleasure."

"Still, you won't get by without them."

"I don't like repeating myself. They're all traitors—by nature."

"You'll get married all the same. A man is far too helpless of a creature to live all alone."

"I despise them."

"You're a liar. And you don't want to admit it. You're always chasing after tarts, because no decent girl has ever shown interest in you. You've never even had a steady girlfriend."

Marat got up from the table and headed toward a gap in the waist-high enclosure that ran round the terrace. He stood by the side of the road and looked out at the stream of traffic flowing in either direction. I knew that he felt very lonely just then, and I felt bad about upsetting him. He was making an effort not to look back. But we knew anyway that he would gladly unburden himself of all the secret and most persistent yearnings that lay at his very core. But Marat kept up his sulking, miserable pose, gazing down the roadway for a long time. I felt sorry for him.

"You didn't have to say that."

"Saian, I'm an idiot."

"You're not the only one. We're all idiots today."

"No, I'm the idiot. I only see lies and trickery, no matter who's talking to me or what they're saying. I can't trust anyone—the only person I love is my grandfather. You know my Toleutai-*ata*—he may be a hero or a wretched fool, I don't know. But besides me there isn't a soul that gives a damn about him. Nobody understands what he's going through. Everything that mattered to him is finished, and he's still going on about the great triumphs of socialism. He's had a hard, miserable life. He thinks that he gave his best years to building some bright future, and he's proud of it. And it just breaks my heart."

"Aidar, there's no point in getting so upset over it. Look at you—how can you be such a baby, such a broken old wretch? Stop it, get up, or go home. Lie down a while, and you'll see—tomorrow everything will be back to normal. Everything will be alright."

"Saian, I feel like my life is over."

"Enough, Aidar. Stop crying. You haven't done anything wrong. You'll see, our time will come, sooner or later."

"You're a good man. You know the meaning of true friendship."

"Don't cry. That's enough."

"Yes, I'll stop. Just give me a second."

But inside I felt terrible, and my tears refused to dry up. Saian earnestly tried to console me.

Almaty, November 1991

One Day in July

"Why don't I help you across?"

"Are you talking about me?"

"Yes."

"I can manage on my own, if that's alright with you."

A car came to an abrupt halt just beside a plain, bare wheelchair.

"You'll get run over."

A young man rolled the wheelchair, occupied by a young woman, back onto the sidewalk. The cars resumed their course. In a moment the roadway had turned once more into an unbroken stream of vehicles.

"Thank you," said the woman.

She was not attractive: a shapeless nose, a flat, broad face, protruding ears.

"You look very lovely."

"Just now?"

"In general."

She blushed.

"You're embarrassing me," she said.

"I could walk you home."

He nearly said 'take you,' but caught himself in time.

"You must be a kind man."

"I'm glad you think so."

The young fellow pulled on the wheelchair.

"It might be better if you pushed from behind."

"Naturally."

Now he walked behind her. The woman was telling him about something. She had narrow, black eyes, a slightly too dark complexion, and a taut upper lip. But the key to human happiness must surely be something else altogether.

"We aren't even properly introduced."

"Sagat," the *jigit* introduced himself.

"Diana."

"Doesn't sound like a Kazakh name."

"Born and bred. My mother must have thought I'd be a beauty queen."

And the woman shrugged her shoulders.

"Well, you are looking lovely today."

Diana gave him a warm smile. A long dress hid her crippled legs. She smiled very politely, as though she knew what was on his mind.

"Yes, it's a hot day. But I always wear long dresses." Sagat became embarrassed.

"Forgive me."

"You mean to say: 'how wretched she must be'?"

She wasn't the least bit dull-witted.

"I always start apologizing when I feel embarrassed. It's an unfortunate habit of mine."

"What do you do? A student?"

"Yes, university."

"And I'm a homebody."

"Don't you get bored?"

"Maybe, every now and then. For the most part I'm pretty content."

"Me, I always feel like I'm all alone."

Diana smiled. That wasn't very smart, thought the young man. I'm sure she knows all about real loneliness.

They stopped at a flower stand, stacked with rows upon rows of baskets full of flowers. When her wheelchair stopped before the section with red roses, Diana's face lit up with pleasure.

"Looks like the Good Lord wanted to make a special day for me."

The young man picked out three flowers and handed her the bouquet in a cellophane wrapper.

"Thank you."

The wheels were set in motion once more and rolled lazily onward, crackling lightly over the sand, strewn here and there on the sidewalk. It seemed that neither would break the silence.

"Why did you decide to help me?" finally said the woman.

Sagat was silent. Only the wheels kept creaking as they rolled along the asphalt.

"Forgive me," she said.

Her voice was breaking.

"Please turn right here."

They turned off the road.

"Here we are."

"There aren't any houses here."

"That's not your problem, is it?"

"Did I offend you?"

They stood beside a savings bank.

"Who gave you the right to pity me?" asked Diana.

"I had no such intention."

"Why do you pity me?" she continued. "Do you happen to know that I'm not alone?"

"I know."

"I have a kind and attentive husband. I have many relatives who care deeply about me; my children are good, responsible people."

The woman started crying. She will never come to terms with it. She will never get used to it—this pity from strangers, from everyone.

The young man didn't know what he ought to do next.

Almaty, 11/12/92

At the Edge

"Maybe you could stand watch outside?" asked Alpamys. Zhunus didn't answer.

"As you like."

"Don't do it, Alpamys, you'll only get in trouble."

"I'm tired."

"Take a vacation, then. Go to Issyk-kul or Burabai."

"I don't want to have any regrets later."

"So what are you going to do?"

"I told you."

"You won't make it, you'll see, and you'll get caught."

A waiter brought their *languette*: a few slices of tenderloin with fries.

"Another round of cognac," said Alpamys.

"Let's order some fruit juice."

"Sure."

The day was hot, and inside the curtains had been drawn on all the windows. Dim lamps were scattered throughout the café. An American crooner was lamenting his lonesome nights. The mood was melancholy. The waiter scribbled something in a notepad, slid it into his pocket, and headed back to his corner, pushing his cart before him.

"What are we drinking to?"

"I don't know."

"Then let's just drink."

Alpamys gulped down his cognac, burning his throat. Cheap consolation, he thought. The next day you go right back to your dreary existence.

"Do you have any regrets?" he asked Zhunus.

"Depends on my mood."

"Me, I've got plenty of regrets."

"Like what?"

"I don't even know where to begin."

"Maybe you made them up?"

"You think they're all invented, with no basis in reality?"

"Right."

"I don't know about that, but they torment me all the same."

"Get married."

"To whom?"

"Plenty of girls out there."

"Plenty."

"So get married. Then your regrets won't feel real."

"People should marry out of love."

"Maybe you'll fall in love—once you're married."

"And what if I don't?"

"Then you'll love your children."

"I'm just tired."

"Another round?"

"Sure."

They called over the waiter. He brought two cognacs and two glasses of juice, unloaded his tray, gathered up the empty dishes, and went away. Alpamys felt sad.

"You really love her?"

"Yes."

The bartender put on a different track. Sure, I love her, but what good is that, thought Alpamys. The music swelled and enveloped them.

"A man never dies," said Alpamys.

"Who knows, maybe not."

They were silent for a while.

"Do you want to die?"

"Careful, you'll get yourself run over."

"We don't have to drink too much."

"Fine."

They crossed the street and hailed a taxi. After a while they turned right and rolled along Dzhandosov. The sun stood directly overhead.

"There it is."

They were going past a large four-story building surrounded with a tall iron fence.

"They've got guards everywhere."

"Maybe I'll get lucky."

"You say you believe in God, so how can you do something like this?"

"I'm just setting things right."

"There's no other way of doing that?"

"Most likely there is, but a daring and dangerous enterprise fires the imagination and builds willpower. Real men take real risks."

"What are you trying to prove? To whom?"

"I've already worked through all the guilt and self-doubt. Now it's time for action."

The car slowed down and stopped at a traffic light. They felt a light breeze. Zhunus rolled down the window as far as it could go. He was tired of his own thoughts. He was starting to get angry with Alpamys.

"Drop this idea, will you? It won't make you rich anyway."

"If you're afraid, we can say good-bye right here."

"Don't be like that, Alpamys. Do you understand what this plan of yours means? Larceny. Crime."

"So what?"

"You'll go to jail. You'll rot there. Nobody will give a damn about you. Don't say afterwards that I didn't warn you."

"Are we going to get another drink?"

"Yes."

"Then let's end this conversation."

"Can't you see, I feel sorry for you?"

"Nobody asked you to feel sorry."

"You'll ruin your life."

"We'll see."

"Drop all this. Let's go to Issyk-kul, the two of us. Swimming, sunbathing, drinking—all the fun things."

Alpamys looked out the window. His face registered nothing but indifference. Zhunus saw that he couldn't do anything for his friend. What's he setting straight, anyway?

"Forgive me, Zhunus," Alpamyr said suddenly.

And he burst into tears, sniffling like a small child.

"Let's drink to our health. Tomorrow we'll forget all of this. If you've got your health and a working noodle—that's about all you need to be happy."

"That's for sure."

After downing his cognac, Alpamys felt lonely. The drink warmed him up. But Zhunus was taking his time with it. *All of it is shot through with that sadness that's always after us,* he thought, and added:

"It is injustice that breeds sadness."

"And sadness is the ultimate form of spiritual yearning."

Almaty, April 2002

The Day the World Collapsed

(*excerpt*)

By Rollan Seisenbaev

To victims of nuclear tests
and other ecological disasters

...

And calamity fell upon the men of Chingis mountains in the summer of '53. It fell in a single stroke ... All at once the children watching over goats and sheep on the outskirts of the *auil* heard fearful cries and shouting and women's wailing. Leaving their charges behind, in the open steppe, they raced home, their bare soles flashing in the dust. None of them has ever seen anything like it: everywhere men and women, young and old, wept and embraced one another, cursing and lamenting and taking leave of one another, as though they would never meet again. All was chaos and confusion: the boys stood frozen in place, marveling at the upheaval that had suddenly and unexpectedly overwhelmed our quiet and lazy *auil*. Maybe a war has broken out? We noted the giant army trucks and soldiers scurrying about everywhere, as though they had just popped out of the ground. I bet it's the Americans, or some other imperialists, conjectured one of us.

"Look at that ... One, two, three ... There's ten wheels on every truck," said Serbikol.

"Not bad ... Ten ... Unbelievable ..." the boys chattered, trying to climb into the cab or in the back at the very least.

"If it's war, then I'm joining the partisans," announced Serbikol, and all of us envied him, because he had said it first. Every one of us imagined himself a soldier, or at the very least some kind of "drummer boy."

"Boys, hit the barracks!" shouted a man with the insignia of a lieutenant-colonel.

"Sir, who are we fighting?" I asked timidly.

"No one's fighting anyone. Cut the chit-chat! Get yourself home on the double; your parents are waiting for you—this is an evacuation!" The officer was irritated.

None of us had the least idea of what an "evacuation" meant, but it was evident that nothing good was going to come of it. An odor of fear and uncertainty clung to that mysterious, hazy word.

Back home, I found grandpa out in the yard, greasing the hubs of our old araba.

"Why don't you give me a hand here?" Grandpa waved me over.

I asked what was going on.

"We're being evicted," he said glumly.

"Where? Why?" I marveled, secretly excited by this sudden shake-up. I was seven, and all summer long I had been stuck in the *auil*, tending sheep. Around the same time I had been reading Mark Twain, and my spirit thirsted for adventure, even if I had to journey to the ends of the earth to find it.

"To the city," grandpa confided grudgingly.

"Then why are you greasing up the araba?"

For some reason my question irritated him.

"City ... city ..." he repeated in a mocking tone. "Everyone's squawking about going down to the city like a bunch of parrots. And what about the animals? Maybe they'll come to the city too? Not me—I'm going up into the mountains. What do you say—are you coming along with me, or will you go with your mother?"

Grandpa fixed me with a piercing gaze, and I had to lower my eyes. I, for one, had no problems with the city. That was where my Au-*apa* lived, my grandmother on my mother's side. She was a stern and imperious woman, and she loved me and treated me like an adult. Three dozen years have passed since that time, but I still remember vividly the evenings when we sat together on a park bench—just the two of us—and spoke to one another, as though we were two equals. She could talk me about all sorts of subjects that were on her mind, including her daughter, my mother, and her son-in-law, my father. It seemed to me that she loved my father even more than she loved her own daughter. She loved him, and she loved me ...

I didn't dare raise my eyes, because I did not know how to tell all of this to grandpa.

"So, you'll be going to the city, then?" I couldn't tell by his voice whether it was a serious question or merely a jeer.

I flushed and said vaguely:

"We'll see what dad thinks ..."

"What's there to see?" snapped grandpa. "Everything is clear as day as it is. No *burkit* are you, good sir ... Fine, go on, I'll manage here without you."

I lingered awkwardly for a few moments, then went into house. Mama and grandma were busy wrapping up bundles—the whole house had been turned upside-down. My little brother got in everyone's way, sniveling and clinging to grandma's skirts. Our baby sister, who was barely a year old then, slept in her tiny crib.

"Why don't you take him outside to play," said mama, looking at my brother.

I took him up in my arms and went out into the yard. For a moment grandpa looked up from his work, but said nothing.

"No *burkit* … no *burkit* …" I parroted grandpa silently. "You're no lion yourself!"

Suddenly, I heard loud voices and a woman's cries, and a handful of people came into our yard.

"What's to become of us! We're done for! All of us!" cried our neighbor, the old woman Bokei.

"They tell me this here bomb has superhuman strength—it'll wipe Chingistau clean off the face of the earth," volunteered old Kabysh.

"This bomb is worse than the one they dropped on Hiroshima. That was atomic—this one's hydrogen," said a man who had been a physics teacher.

"*Ai*, Moldabergen, what will we do?" took up Bokei once more.

"We'll pack our bags," said grandpa curtly.

"Where's your son?" Bokei asked all of a sudden.

"Where should he be? At work … They've got the army down at the district committee," explained Kabysh.

"Whatever the authorities decide—that's how it'll be. Their word is our law," nodded the physics teacher. He had the reputation of a judicious and honest man. And he was no coward—he had gone off to war as a private and came back a lieutenant …

Suddenly Kabysh saw a problem: "What will happen to the animals?"

Grandpa gave him a mocking glance: "What do you think? We'll drive them into the mountains. Or did you plan on bringing your sheep with you to the city? An ass with a load of sheep—that's what they'll call you in the city."

"No, it wouldn't do to take them to the city," Kabysh agreed.

"Don't you have anything better to do than hang about here?" snapped grandpa all of a sudden. "We'll be getting on the road any day now, and you're here talking nonsense!"

"Right you are, right you are," stammered the old woman Bokei, and she hurried off, moaning and sniffling all the while.

Suddenly the loudspeaker that hung from a post in the middle of the *auil* crackled to life, and a woman's tinny voice announced:

"Esteemed comrades! Please assemble in the main square in thirty minutes to meet with representatives of the evacuation committee …"

The square was soon flooded with men. I stood beside grandpa inside the restless crowd.

Men in fatigues came up the podium, followed by district supervisors, and I saw my father among them. He looked tired—his eyes were red from lack of sleep—but when he finally spoke he seemed calm and confident. I cannot remember what he said to us that day, nor do I remember the words of the other speaker, an older officer with two stars on his epaulets—that same lieutenant-colonel who had chased us off earlier in the day.

In the evening father brought him and two other officers to supper at our house. From their terse conversation I could gather that the villagers were to be evacuated to the nearby city Aiaguz, but that whoever wanted could also go Semipalatinsk, the district capital. The old folks were allowed to go into the Chingis mountains with the animals. So that was why the giant army trucks had come to our village.

In the morning the lieutenant-colonel advised the villagers to take along only basic necessities and to bar the windows with bales of hay, and he reassured them that in a month's time everyone would be free to go home.

"For now, all of you will receive an allowance of 500 rubles per household. Please go to the district committee office to claim your money," he concluded.

For most of the villagers, five hundred "Malenkov" rubles was a good deal of money. The villagers proudly signed their names in the register, drawn up by the committee treasurer Talgat, and yet they looked away as they took their money and hurried out of the hall.

Only the old bachelor Duisehan, who was thought to be something of a village idiot, categorically refused to accept the money.

"Duisehan is not taking handouts!" he shouted angrily and left the meeting.

Some were amused and others outraged by this gesture. Everyone knew that Duisehan was practically a pauper and lived on whatever he could get for an odd job: digging or cleaning wells, helping at harvest time, etc. A more settled lifestyle did not suit his tastes …

"Aren't you a proud one! If this ragamuffin won't take free money, then I will," proposed Otegen, a retired policeman.

"Sure, you'll take whatever you can get your grubby hands on! Shameless! You've got no fear of God!" pounced the old woman Bokei.

"Your god's not handing out cash lately," snarled Otegen, more to himself. He had been a tyrant and a bully in his days, and he knew well enough that his fellow villagers had not forgotten it …

At night, when everything had settled down, I came up to my father.

"Papa," I said, "I'm not going to Aiaguz."

"You want to go to Au-*apa* in Semipalatinsk?" he asked.

"No … I'll go with grandpa," I stammered.

Father looked at me strangely and said nothing.

"I want to be with grandpa," I repeated.

THE END OF THE WORLD. 1953. AUGUST 17. 18:12. EVERYTHING BEGINS IN KAZAKHSTAN!

So, this was the end of the world prophesied by that wanderer. What happens to the human soul after death? I felt something like an electric shock pass through my entire body, from the very tip of my head down to my feet. I wanted to live! I was seven, and it was the first time I thought seriously about death, which until that moment had occupied no place in my consciousness. For the first time I REALLY felt the menacing approach of the old faceless crone with the scythe ... Tomorrow, maybe even today, my soul would stand before the seat of heavenly judgment ... A black cloud of death hung over me—and over everything and everyone around me ...

The time of departure had passed, but the trucks were not ready, and the lieutenant-colonel was growing impatient. Mother had kissed father good-bye, and now she was trying to tell him something in a rapid monologue. Finally the trucks started up. Some were on their way to Aiaguz—a mysterious place, as far as I was concerned—and others would go on to distant Semipalatinsk. The old men and women set out for the Chingis mountains.

I sat at the reins. Death hadn't gone off with the trucks on their way to Aiaguz or Semipalatinsk ... it lay in wait for us at the heart of Chingistau ... I was frightened, but I also wanted more than anything to be a *burkit*! So that I might look bravely in the eyes of my grandfather, the lion! So that my mother and father, my little brother and baby sister could be proud of me! And also Kenzhe ...

Our araba led the way. I turned my head and saw a long procession of carriages and old men driving their flocks. Suddenly, a car pulled up next to us, and my father and the lieutenant-colonel stepped out of it.

"Our soldiers will go ahead of you and look for a camp site," said the officer. The old man scowled.

"So they know our mountains better than us?"

"Well ... they've got a better idea ..." said the officer vaguely and laughed. Grandpa's words had annoyed him.

"Right—all you've got is good ideas, and we've got no ideas of our own. Your idea is to kill us all." Grandpa spit on the ground. Grandma, sitting just beside him, reached out cautiously and touched his shoulder.

"Have you gone completely mad?" she said in a hoarse whisper. "You don't give a damn about yourself, at least you can think of your son. Keep talking like this and they'll pack you away—and all the rest of us along with you."

"Quiet, woman ..." It seemed as though Grandpa was about to fly into a real fury. "This is our land. I want to hear what they intend to do with it."

He was a quick-tempered but fair-minded man. At the end of the twenties, when Chingistau was in the grips of famine, he had gone to live in the city. But

our land. I figured he didn't know a single real thing about us. He probably hadn't even seen a Kazakh before that time. But suddenly the colonel came up to grandpa and put his arms around him.

"I hear you, father," he said, "and I understand you. All of us have suffered. And we have suffered more than any other nation on this earth. We have lost the father of all nations, comrade Stalin, who had led us to victory over the fascists. And now another threat hangs over us. Haven't you heard that the Americans have already dropped a nuclear bomb on Japan? And now they are threatening us—and we must be prepared to meet their threat. We don't want to fight anyone, but we must always stand ready for when they come. Can't you see that? Yes, we are conducting tests, but all measures have been taken to ensure the safety of the population. This is why we have asked you to leave your *auil*. It would not be fair to say that we are chasing you off to die. This is a necessary precaution—we want to save our country from an American invasion ..."

Grandpa listened and frowned. Then he made a sharp about-face and walked back to his araba. Father tousled my hair and slapped me on the shoulder.

"Go on," he said. "Go and help your grandpa and grandma like we agreed."

I nodded in accord, and involuntarily looked up at the skies: maybe an American bomb was already on its way to kill us? But the sky was clear and peaceful, without a single cloud.

"What'll you have to eat?" grandma asked my father. "We've got some flour we could give you."

"No need. We're supplied with canned products," replied father. "Don't worry about me. Just do whatever the army people tell you ..."

"If you end up starving, you can eat the chickens. I left them for you ..." Grandpa snapped his whip, ignoring father's last instructions, and we set off again.

By sunrise the mountains were once more swarming with soldiers.

"Where did they come from?" wondered grandpa.

"It's like they're crawling out of the earth," said old Arham with a tremor in his voice.

Some of the soldiers came up to us, and one of them—probably their commander—announced:

"They will start in half an hour. At the time of the explosion you will be covered with your *kiyizs* and you will stay that way until further notice. The fires are to be put out immediately."

The soldiers were already putting out our fires. Their curt, abrupt commands had broken up the morning calm. People were pulling out their *kiyizs*, banding together into small groups and making ready to take cover. Kenzhe lay between me and grandma. Her delicate face looked drawn, and her large eyes seemed frozen with fear. I noticed that her long lashes were trembling. Grandpa was muttering a prayer. Grandpa had pulled the blanket over my head, and I tried to peek out, which made her angry.

The soldiers scurried about us. I heard their cracked, hoarse voices. Suddenly, the commander called out in a loud voice:

"Attention! Attention! Everyone down! Nobody move!"

And—the earth rocked softly beneath us. It seemed to me as though it were an eternal crib that would rock us to sleep. But all of a sudden it shuddered and heaved up, pummeling us on the legs, chests, and faces from below; I felt grandma's grip slacken; the earth bucked and reared like an unbroken stallion; the steppes and the mountains strained to keep from crumbling. Peeking out from under my *kiyiz*, I saw a fantastic mushroom fill the sky and all about it a fiery light show, with wild and violent colors. Fear and astonishment gripped me—I had never seen anything like it. The mountains groaned, and giant boulders came rolling down from their peaks; trees strained and shrieked … and suddenly I could hear another sound—a desperate, piercing cry—rising over the hellish cacophony. To this day I cannot name this fearful sound. A little girl in a white dress ran down the mountain, ran beside the bounding stones. I don't remember how I managed to get out from under the *kiyiz*. I stood, frozen in place, looking on as she ran. The fiery mushroom rose up over us; flashes of light blinded me; where was she running to, this little girl, over the quaking earth? What was I to do? Her cries pierced my ears. Or did I only imagine that she was crying out? Maybe she only stretched her mouth wide open, but no sound came from it, and maybe she was running not into the steppe, but up into the mountains and the thundering boulders leapt aside to make way for her.

I thought: "She will die. I must save her; I must run after her."

I cried out "Kenzhe! Kenzhe!" I ran after her, and suddenly a thought came to me: "She must have gone mad!" Shocked by this sudden revelation, I tripped and fell to the ground. At that very moment a great stone flew over me, and I understood that Allah had saved me from a sure death. Kenzhe had gone mad … gone mad … I had nearly caught up to her. Her narrow shoulders trembled, and tears streamed down her face as she ran, and now I could really hear her cry: A-a-ah! Suddenly bursts of fire came up from the earth. I caught up to Kenzhe and we fell to the ground. I heard the heavy rumble of boots drawing near. Someone threw a *kiyiz* over us, and a voice shouted: "Down! Lie still!" Kenzhe pressed my hand softly.

"Don't worry," I whispered, but she said nothing. To this day I have not forgotten the touch of her moist hand …

Once again the earth trembled. It convulsed in a fit of agony, and my heart beat wildly in response, and my soul was frozen with fear. I forgot about Kenzhe; I forgot about everything in the world—the only thing I knew was that the world had collapsed on top of me, and that I was going to die under its ruins. I thought only of myself: death stood over me with its axe held high, and the blade would now strike down on my defenseless neck. I could feel my consciousness slipping away, and in this daze I felt the hand of Kenzhe grow cold. "She must have died," I realized, as my consciousness slowly flickered back to life.

Under the *kiyiz*, in utter and terrible darkness, I lay beside the dead Kenzhe, my body bathed in cold sweat. A mere boy, I suddenly realized that I was in love with this poor sickly and sickly child. I tried to draw my face close to hers so that I might kiss her for the first and last time.

"Down! Lie still!" the same menacing voice shouted over me. But I managed to stretch my neck and press my lips to her forehead. I heard another shout, but it sounded muffled, and I understood that the soldier had also hidden himself under a *kiyiz*. And it seemed as though the end of the world had come.

We came down the mountain slowly, as we were told, and traveled a long way along the steppe, camping by night on the banks of small rivers and streams.

When early one morning we finally reached home, we discovered that the *auil* was deserted—we were the first to come back. Actually, a brigade of soldiers arrived ahead of us, with orders to clear out the wells before the villagers' return. This was an unnecessary precaution—soon new lakes would form in the district with dead, radioactive water. Those that swam in these waters, out of ignorance or bravado, received a deadly dose of radiation and soon died. In time the people understood the danger and avoided those false waters like the plague.

The old men, who came down with us from the mountains, took their leave, and each went his way along the wide streets of the village. Grandpa drove his grey mare to our spacious yard at the center of the *auil*. At first he went slowly, but seeing a group of soldiers hovering over our well, he snapped his *kamshi* over the horse's ear and our old araba went flying at full tilt until it reached the house.

Grandpa was shouting, brandishing his *kamshi*, and tearing the buckets from the soldiers' hands. The soldiers didn't know what this was about; meanwhile, someone was shouting at them from inside the well: "Hey you, lazy asses! Get these buckets in here. What's going on up there?"

Grandpa looked down into the well, and his face grew fierce. He shouted: "Why you miserable *kafir*! Get out of there this minute! You've spoiled all of my water!"

The soldiers pulled up a young private, and all of them stood gaping at grandpa.

"Who asked you, filthy *kafirs*, to jump in my well?"

The adults were talking about the coming days, of the threat of poverty and the fear of the atomic bomb—the American threat. Father was trying to alert the old folks to the American menace, and he chopped the air with his hand—which made me think that he was only repeating what the soldiers had told him.

And I remembered the mountains—that terrible explosion, when it seemed as though the chord that held the earth tied to the sun might snap, and we would be hurled into the depths of an unfathomable universe, like those thundering boulders that rolled down the mountains, frightening men and animals. I remembered how the horses scattered away from fright, and how the old folks spent days wandering after them. I remembered how the earth was pulled out from under my feet, and how I fell and pressed myself to its cool and damp body. And I also remembered how she ran alongside the bounding boulders—little Kenzhe, who had lost her mind from fright and grief.

Kamshiger

(excerpt)

By Oralhan Bokeev

Beneath the moonlight—beneath the moonlight gleams a solitary white yurt, and upon its threshold stoops a woman in black—a widow.

Beneath the moonlight—beneath the moonlight a steppe spreads wide, a ruddy steppe, made brazen by the moonbeam. Kind she is and generous, our steppe, the mother of all the *batyrs* that cling to it, wearied by strife, that sleep the eternal sleep—the final refuge, the parting song. O Kazakh steppe!

The wind that blows from the Tuye-Tas gorge howls like a pack of hounds. It is a mournful and vicious wind that could throw a rider from the saddle. Its wanton kiss sucks the color from a man's lips and turns the face stony. The wind that blows from the Tuye-Tas gorge …

Two mountain peaks pierce the skies like two blazing spears—a fearsome chasm spreads open between them, dotted at the bottom with a handful of larch trees. This is the gorge of Tuye-Tas: the mutinous brook Sharyktybulak blasphemes at the heavens, spitting up its white foam flakes, and the howling wind surges up the frigid rock wall, desperate to break free, only to crash against the pitch-black crag that overhangs the gorge like an eternal watchman. The cliff resembles a great angry camel, and that is why people had called that place Tuye-Tas, the gorge of Tuye-Tas.

A modest yurt had found shelter from the wind at the very foot of the cliff. No other human dwelling could ever spring up in that place. On every side stern cliffs, gloomy rocks, and mighty trees tower over the solitary yurt. And it seems as though life here had come to a standstill many centuries ago—here, in this remote and sullen place, forgotten by time, a wild corner of a different world that lives according to its own, unfathomable laws …

Every now and again a woman, wrapped in a shawl, slips down to the brook to fetch water, and just as swiftly retraces her path back to the yurt. Then all is silence once more. A silence thick as the morning fog … A silence that seems to lie in wait … A wild and desolate place …

Only the throaty rumble of the brook and the menacing whoop of the eagle owl may be heard there. In the spring this place was suffused with the sweet scent of the mountain tulip, but now the summer is passed, and the autumn has seared the flowers with its icy breath—they have withered and the grasses have browned. Now the bitter scent of the sagebrush holds sway over the mountains—the scent of drought and decay.

Pause for a moment, traveler, and you will see a hardy steed, tied to a post beside the yurt—so great is he that it seems he could lift his head and touch his lips to the stars, or knock the earth from its orbit with a stamp of his hind legs.

From nightfall he stands in this place, and later in the night he grazes in the glade just behind the yurt. In the dark of night one could see the glimmer of a fire through the tears in the *kiyiz*, and wisps of smoke rising over the *tundik*. The wind of Tuye-Tas sweeps up the smoke and carries it to some unknown place—the smoke of human life, rich with the scent of boiled meat. And when the star Sholpan comes to stand over the cliff the door of the dwelling opens with a plaintive sigh, and the owner of the horse steps over the threshold—a barrel-chested, big-boned giant. The *jigit* casts a long gaze at the moon, sighs, and walks toward his steed. His eyelids seem heavy, but his frowning eyes take in every grass blade that stands before him.

The sky grows pale, and there is silence all about him, while the moon gallops across the skies, trying to keep pace with the fading night.

The skies are silent. The stones are silent. All is plunged into a deep sleep—the black woods, the blue mountains, and the grey yurt. O traveler, it is the deep sleep of daybreak.

His heavy *kamshi* with a brass tip hangs on the wall. It was woven from twelve strong leather cords. The *kamshi* is a life-giver, a *kamshiger's* salvation. Without it no man could find glory. No man could fill the cauldron with fragrant meat. He had given a heifer and a calf to its maker, and his *kamshi* hangs always in a place of honor.

But what's this? A drop of moisture appears on the brass tip, it swells and sways and at last falls to the ground … One after another, drops of liquid fall from the tip—even though the handle and the cord remain dry. What sort of wonder is this? Where do these warm, heavy drops come from, scented with almond and mare's milk?

Doskei lies still, and it seems to him that it is heady *kimiz* dripping down to him from a wondrous *torsyk*. He lies still and the drops of heavenly *kimiz* soothe his burning eyes, and his heart is made glad, and he would tell his wife about this marvelous *kimiz*.

But she sleeps, dreaming a dream of a spring song. He can hear her low breath, and he wants to turn to her, embrace her, and tell her about the miracle, but it is as though a wicked spell had been cast over him, and he cannot so much as raise a finger.

"Kamka!" he whispers to her. But the sleeping woman cannot hear him.

"Kamka! Kamka!" he cries out in terror. "Kamka! Kamka, wake up!"

Nothing but silence. A dead, funereal silence. A blood-curdling hush.

But the *kimiz* keeps on dripping from the *kamshi* … The liquid runs down from his eyes, over his cheeks—a thick and heady wonder.

"Come what may …" thinks Doskei, and parts his lips.

All at once he is seized with terror and disgust. Blood! The salty scent of fresh human blood rushes into his nostrils. Blood!

"Blood … it is blood. Whose blood is it, Kamka? Can't you tell me? Kamka, speak! Speak!"

His whole body shuddered and he opened his eyes. His face was drenched in tears. Kamka slept soundly by his side—his cries did not wake her. Comforted by this thought, Doskei sprang to his feet and went out of the yurt.

Before midnight the skies were pristine—but now leaden clouds hung over him and a gray drizzle tapped ceaselessly the earth about his feet. His bay, grown darker from the rain, stood with his neck bent low, shaking his head every now and then, as though trying to shake off a toothache.

Sharytybulak has overflowed its banks, and the cliffs, swathed in gloomy dusk, stand brooding silently, resigned to the arrival of autumn rains. The earth lies still, worn out by the plentiful, hot summer.

Doskei untied his horse and brought it under the broad canopy of a larch tree. He picked up the saddle that lay just outside the door, soaking in the rain.

Kamka slept, her breath deep and even, her limbs tossed carelessly. Suddenly Doskei was seized by a fit of anger.

"Enough laying about!" he shouted. "Get up, I'm hungry!"

He dropped down beside the *dastarkhan*, his nostrils quivering with inexplicable rage. Frightened and confused, Kamka hastily warmed the goat meat left over from their supper and set it before her husband, but he did not even touch it.

"There's a hair. Get the hair out of the meat," he said hoarsely, and tossed aside the bowl. Once more he lay down, pulling the heavy *shekpen* made of camel's hair over his head, but in the next instant he threw off the *shekpen*, as though it would smother him, and began gasping for air. "O Lord! Oof!" he exclaimed again and again, his gasps resembling sobs.

Kamka had never seen her husband act this way, and so she crouched beside the brazier, not daring to question him. She looked on with tenderness and timidity as Doskei kept tossing and turning, his face darkened with rage.

"Kamka!" he said at last, raising himself up in bed, his voice wheezing. "Kamka, where is my *kamshi*?"

"Where?" she repeated. "It's there, over your head, where it always hangs."

"Throw it out!"

"What for? What are you saying?" She looked at him in astonishment, but he said nothing more, and so she rose, took the whip down from the wall and set it down next to the saddle. Then she dropped to the floor and buried her face in her hands.

Kamshi! His heavy *kamshi* with a brass tip, woven from twelve cords of leather. He had given a heifer and a calf for it, and he never regretted it, because the *kamshi* is a *kamshiger's* only friend, his salvation. Without it, no man could find glory. No man could fill the blackened cauldron with fragrant meat. Who could endure this wicked and lonely life without *kamshi*? A *kamshi* made him strong and invincible; it was at his side during his boldest, most daring raids, but now … now it seems to him lifeless, worthless … He wants it thrown out—but without it, how will he eat? How will he live?

He has ordered it to be thrown out—he has humiliated his *kamshi*, and debased himself. It is as though with a single act he has wiped out his whole life—a life full of risk, adventure, and struggle. And he had loved that life—the shrieks of bullets overhead, the frenzied breath of the chase, the sweet joy of gazing down on a vanquished enemy.

But now he has thrown out, humiliated, cursed his *kamshi*, all because he saw blood in a dream! Hadn't he seen plenty of blood in real life? Hadn't he always said to his *jigit* that he could not bear to taste bread that was not won with risk and mortal danger?

He gnashed his teeth, fell on his side, and lay as stiff as a dead man, his eyes half-closed. He stayed this way until noontime, and it was impossible to tell whether he slept or was awake.

A terrible fear seized Kamka, because she had never before seen her husband in this state. She sensed disaster drawing near.

"O god, he will die …" she whispered, gazing into the flames of the brazier, and listening to the crackle of its twigs. For the first time since her wedding day she felt abandoned and lonely, and for the first time since that day she felt a yearning to see her *auil*, to see the people she once knew. She remembered her mother's kind hands, and tears rolled down her cheeks.

Six *jigit* came through the low doorway, coughing, spitting and shaking the dust from their cloaks—and the woman rose up to meet them, stifling her tears. All six were strapping young men from the Karatay clan that lived on the other side of Tuye-Tas.

"Where is Doseke?" they asked, not seeing the giant Doskei, laid out by the wall and resembling a sleeping bear.

"There he is," said the woman quietly.

that someone below should lift his head and see the horsemen, Allah forbid! But luck is on their side today—no one has seen them.

"They're sucking those sheep like a bunch of leeches," smirked Doskei and gave a quick signal with his *kamshi*. Soundlessly, the *jigit* slipped down the mountainside and the red pebbles, rustling like lizards in the brush, streamed after them. Soon the horsemen disappeared in the thicket that grew along the coast.

The day was unusually tranquil—it would be madness to launch a raid in broad daylight. Doubtless, the men of the village were well armed and could easily repel a handful of *kamshiger*: there were only seven of them, including Doskei, who now stood watch. But hunger and impatience, joining in a single force, had robbed the *jigit* of their usual prudence. Doskei watched as his comrades, coming to the edge of the *auil*, burst from the thicket, their bodies leaning close to their horses' necks.

The *auil's* horses grazed in the marshy coastal meadows, among patches of bulrush and cattail. Sensing danger at the approach of strangers, the horses scattered in every direction. Only a small band was left in place, locked in by a lake on one side and a sheer cliff on another. The *jigit* drove this band to the Marak pass, and as Doskei looked on, he couldn't help admiring the horses: there were broad-chested riding horses, fiery, unbroken colts, and slender palfreys with their swan's necks. The Kerey may well boast of strong, proud horses!

Doskei looked in the direction of the *auil* and saw that the horses were beginning to scatter, pushing off one another with their rumps, and that his comrades could not hold them together. He was a sharp and experienced watchman, and he would not think of letting another take his place, but this clumsy spectacle filled him with rage.

"Hurry! Hurry!" he whispered to no one in particular. "Will they hurry up, the fools!"

But at this very moment he heard the desperate, horror-stricken cries:

"*Karatay*! *Karatay*! *Kamshiger*! Horse thieves!"

Ah, if only they hadn't raised the alarm, he could have driven off the whole pack! Those snotnoses had only to get as far as the mountain pass, and they couldn't even manage that much. He could have done it alone, all of it …

But there was no time for it. A moment later six horsemen burst out of the *auil* in pursuit.

Doskei wasn't worried—he had seen far worse in his time. Proud and composed, he stood in the pursuers' path.

In their haste, the villagers had left behind their clubs and were only armed with whips—luck was smiling on Doskei.

The horsemen came at him like an avalanche, but just before they reached him Doskei lunged his horse to the side, and the pursuers flew past him. Howling with laughter and calling on all his ancestors, Doskei raced after them, burst into their midst and managed to snatch all six whips from his hapless

All the while Doskei never uttered a word. Unhurriedly he took off his coat, rubbed his right shoulder, and swung his arm a few times to get the blood flowing. Sitting down on a rock, he reached over and snapped off a reed. Suddenly he sprung to his feet—his hand clutched an empty sheath.

"Devil! I lost my knife out there!" he spat out, and instantly six hands held out to him six daggers.

Doskei chuckled, took one of the daggers without looking up at its owner, split the reed, and set about picking his teeth.

"Wait here for me," he spoke up suddenly.

"Where are you going?"

"Where? Back there. I've never yet come back empty-handed from the *Kerey*."

"We're going with you. Whoever burned his lips on milk will be blowing on water—we won't make the same mistake twice," argued the *jigit*.

"No," Doskei cut them off, all the while picking his teeth. "Now we couldn't drive off a whole pack, with the *auil* up in arms. I will try to steal the watchman's steed."

"Doseke, take us with you," the *jigit* whined.

"What? You couldn't handle an old woman, let alone a pack of horses! You want to let me down a second time, you wet-tailed mules! Sit here and don't make a sound!" Doskei shouted scornfully.

There was nothing they could do or say. A moment later Doskei was galloping away.

———————

By the time they reached Black Korgan it had started snowing a wet snow mixed with rain. A heavy darkness lay all about them like a thick blanket—there wasn't a light or a glimmer to be seen anywhere. A black, indifferent night, a wild and desolate place …

Soon the snow turned into a snowstorm. Wind whipped their faces, sucked the last shreds of warmth from their sleeves, crawled under the collar. The horses huddled together, their steps became sluggish.

And the path grew more and more difficult. A path? The trail had long vanished under a blanket of snow, and they continued their trek, guided by little more than guesswork and intuition. Could it be that they had drifted off the path long ago? Doskei stayed at the head of the band, the stolen horse behind him. The rest of the *jigit* followed them like a wolf pack, in single file. Stumbling and falling, on they went, knowing neither how long they had traveled nor where they were likely to end. Where were they going? And why—when the path has long vanished? Why kept moving forward—if there was no longer a forward or backward …? Perhaps they were moving farther and farther away from their homes?

remembered him and despised him. But what did he—a man full of strength and courage—care about another man's grudge? No, he had no enemies—no worthy enemies, at any rate … In all of his life he had never met a true adversary—one that was fierce, clever, and cunning. There were bloody fights, to be sure, but there was no enemy …

Whom then had he battled all his life?

The path lay along the edge of the precipice—it was no wider than a hair's breadth, and sharper than a knife blade … The path over the chasm of Syuk-shat.

The men led their horses on foot—one had to be especially careful here: a single step in the wrong direction would send you tumbling down to the very bottom, down to the brook Sharyktybulak, and there—on the craggy rocks—you would find your final rest. The locals called this narrow pass "the bridge of righteous men" because they believed that whoever is killed here would forever remain a sinner in the eyes of the faithful.

Doskei walked at the head, and behind him went his hapless comrades, like a pack of jackals. Beads of sweat stood out on his forehead—he groped for the path with his hands, and with the handle of his *kamshi*.

"Hold!" was all he had time to cry out as he slipped down into the abyss, and the cliffs of Altai echoed again and again his final warning.

And once more a terrible silence settled over the mountains. Six "righteous men" reached the other side of the "bridge to paradise."

Doskei was badly hurt, but his mind and his memory remained clear and sharp.

His cracked skull was bandaged with twigs of willow soaked in brine—the twigs were wound tightly and caused him terrible pain, even though they were lined in places with patches of chintz. The veins on his temples swelled and turned purple. His hands trembled …

Still the mighty *kamshiger* would hardly let this wound keep him indoors—he would have kept on with his raids, despite the pain, but his right hip had been shattered in the fall, and he refused to call for a bone-setter. "It's useless," he muttered, "a doctor couldn't do a thing with this. Useless … useless …"

He asked for the hide of a freshly killed ewe—with a shimmering lining of fat beneath the skin—and had it stuffed full of plantain leaves. This he wrapped tightly about his hip, tied it together with thick woolen thread—and it seemed to the *kamshiger* that the pain had subsided some …

During that time he had a steady stream of visitors. The *aksakal* and *karasakal* of the Karatay clan came to see the brave *jigit*, along with relatives and former comrades. All of them begged Doskei to put off his solitary ways and rejoin his people, before some greater calamity could befall him. But the

but a weak smile lit up her wearied face. Quietly he crawled over to her and flared his nostrils, sucking in the long-familiar scent of her skin. Then, with great effort, he pulled himself up to his knees and pulled the *kamshi* from the wall.

The hide that held his leg had come loose at one end, and from under it came the heavy stench of rotting flesh. He stood still for a moment. His face contorted in a grimace—either from pain or from the nauseating smell. Then, regaining his composure, he crawled forward on his knees, using the handle of his *kamshi* as a support and grinding his teeth from the unbearable strain.

Reaching the beam that held up the yurt, he lifted himself up to his feet and hobbled toward the door. Finally, gathering all his strength, he pushed open the door—the October chill burst into the yurt.

The *kamshiger* straggled outside, and stood still for some time, trying to catch his breath.

Moving about on his knees as before, he gathered up the ox hides spread outside the yurt and stacked them into a neat pile. He had collected these hides over many years—the hides of stolen oxen. Groaning from pain, nearly losing consciousness, he fell on the stack of hides.

Then he untied the thread wrapped around his leg and pressed his fingers into the injured hip—it was soft as dough, and seeing the deep depression left by his fingers, Doskei twisted his lips in a bitter smile and shook his head. He saw that his horse had turned its head to him and seemed ready to leap, to bellow its triumphant cry, to rear up on its hind legs, and to carry him off, away from his pursuers, from his troubles, from his illness, from death itself.

"God's creature, you understand everything," thought Doskei fondly, but in the next moment he leapt to his feet, as though stung. Some unknown force lifted him up and would not let him fall. Gnashing his teeth, he swung his *kamshi* over the stack of hides and split them open down to the last one, as though he had struck them with a sword.

His body swayed form side to side. He gazed out to the distant snowy peaks, to the deep chasms hidden in the fog, and his whole life passed before his eyes.

He wept. He stood, leaning on his good leg, his body racked with sobs. Then, as though a mighty oak uprooted in the storm, he fell to the ground.

The sky grew red. The dawn was near. A strange sky and a strange dawn— because the mighty *kamshiger* had gone from the world.

The strongest of the *jigit* could not unclench his fist that gripped the *kamshi*. He had gone to his death with his *kamshi* in hand, and his face frozen with the strain of his final moments.

The elders decided that his wrist ought to be cut off so that the *kamshi* could be set free, but Kamka would not hear of it.

"He has no son that could inherit his arms," she cried, sobbing. "They were inseparable in life, let them remain together in heaven."

Reason's Ardent Struggle

(*excerpt*)

By Tulen Abdikov

Today I found another letter. I had sworn to myself to stay away from the bottom drawer of the table that sits out in the hallway, but finally I couldn't resist—I slipped my hand inside and … I must be one of those miserable souls that chase after their own doom. Since morning some persistent and unaccountable impulse had drawn me there. At first I resisted … But by noontime I literally sprinted down the corridor toward the table. And here I am, slumped against the wall, panting for breath, like some delirious animal caught in a hunter's noose. A letter is clutched in my fist.

The truth is, I am terrified of these letters. To me they are nothing less than a challenge to a fight to the death. I'm not looking to fight anyone. If this last letter hadn't come I could have enjoyed a brief rest in the battle against that force of darkness, which I battle day in and day out with little hope of triumph. I had yearned for a rest, for relief. I needed to regain my moral strength, to brace myself for the coming battle. But my invisible foe came at me with a treacherous lunge. Here was his second letter …

My undiscovered companion! Since I had had no news of you, I was obliged to compose the following letter. I ask you, once more, to forgive me the indiscretion of reading your intimate journal without leave.

Reading it, however, I was struck by your lopsided faith—if I may say so—in man's goodness, but not his wickedness. To my mind, it would be more accurate and more equitable to believe in both. Is it possible that you cannot see our world resting evenly on these two pillars? If the wagon of this life is pulled along by two shafts, then surely one of these must be evil. And yet this evil is not so malevolent in its essence as you suppose, nor is it the sole cause of man's misfortunes. Consider death: surely it is to be counted among the greatest evils of this world. But think, my friend, what life might be without death. If the old and sick did not die off, if wicked men, criminals and cruel tyrants lived on indefinitely—why, it would be a true hell on earth! Indeed, it is death and death alone that spins the flywheels of this life, that sustains and rejuvenates it.

Finally, if men had no will for murder, how might they defend themselves against bloodthirsty predators—of the two-legged variety? This also: most of us fear the venomous snake—and yet, countless life-saving drugs and remedies are made from its poison. Will you tell me, then, whether this deadly poison is "good" or "evil"? No, my friend—it would be foolish to brand the things of this life with a single brand. We must judge this or that thing as good or evil only insofar as it bears us some direct harm or benefit, and neither quality will be found in its pure form, free from the admixture of self-interest.

As for lies and deception—we know, of course, that these qualities are everywhere scorned by "decent men." And yet, if Lady Lie could speak, she would say something to this effect: "My dear fellows! If today you are alive and well, and so confident in your moral standing, is it not thanks to my handicraft? If at every turn you were obliged to speak the truth and nothing but the truth—why, you would have torn each other into bloody bits ages ago! I have saved your hide many times, and I will do it again and again for years to come. The truth is, you wouldn't last a day without me." Indeed, my undiscovered friend, there is little we could say in response to Lady Lie, because her words are fundamentally true.

In your journal you also make frequent mention of decency and purity. For your sake, I would like to relate a story that I had heard from an acquaintance.

Once a certain reasonably intelligent and quite handsome little lady deceived her husband. As luck would have it, the poor thing contracted a venereal disease. Let us not dwell too long on the particulars or preachy morals: suffice it to say that the facts of marital infidelity have become commonplaces in our times. Perhaps if this adulterous wife had followed the usual route—that is, kept all her secrets and sought treatment—she would soon have been cured and that would be the end of the story. These days a solution to this sort of trouble is simple and readily available. However, haunted by her guilt, our little lady imagined herself unworthy of her supposedly dishonored husband—and so she hanged herself. In a single stroke she had widowed her husband and orphaned her child. What shall we say to that, my dear fellow?

The deceived husband was inconsolable. Most of all he was crushed by his wife's monstrous error: believing her husband to be the purest of men, and seeing no way to redeem herself in his eyes, she could find no other recourse but the noose. And yet her husband genuinely loved her, and was ready to forgive her all sorts of indiscretion. Moreover, he was fully aware of his own foibles and by no means counted himself the paragon of virtue.

What am I driving at? Only that she could have gone on living with all the banal errors and usual shortcomings, rather than yearning for absolute purity and decency. "We could never be happy again …" What delusion! What rank superstition! These are the things that ruin lives and undermine the world. What do we hope to gain by poisoning our minds with some imagined ideal of absolute purity that has no place in the nature of things?

So much for the little tale, my undiscovered friend. Did you enjoy it?

To attain happiness, all we have to do is form a clear idea of who we are and what sort of thing we are. However painful it may be, we must acknowledge that we are no saints, but mere mortals born in sin and therefore thoroughly contaminated by vice. Unless we humbly accept this truth, we shall never be free of the needless, senseless, and interminable agony of the soul's self-flagellation.

When I think of these things I sometimes imagine that if we could only put out our hand the bluebird of happiness would alight there, proudly beating its great wings. If only we could be free of the superstition of purity and blameless chastity.

I can only hope that you will heed my advice—and may the bluebird come down and alight in your outstretched hand.

I remain your well-wisher, and I sincerely hope that you will not deny me a response.

Your secret pal.

I remember that as I read the final lines of the letter its pages fluttered in my trembling fingers. "Calm down! Get a hold of yourself …" I remember saying. But a storm of indignation was raging in my soul. My thoughts, like animals panicked in an earthquake, scattered in every direction, and I had trouble keeping my attention focused. Gradually, however, I was able to tamp down the confusion—I even made an effort to reason with myself about some of the matters discussed in the letter.

But a shadow of some vague terror hung over my heart like a storm cloud. Someone was certainly out to get me. Someone was trying to worm his way into the innermost chamber of my soul. What for? Merely to torment me? Or had he hatched some dark and wicked scheme …?

After a time I was once more calm enough to consider carefully the stranger's latest missive. To be sure, some of the arguments were not without merit. But that was precisely what made them so dangerous. The beast of doubt had been let loose in my soul. It comes as a bearer of truth, and a meek countenance is its chief snare. Yet it brings no truth, but only lies, cloaked in a thin layer of truth—and that is a great danger, indeed. The blackest villain is the one that comes in the guise of a humble philosopher—he is a fearsome adversary.

At the same time I saw clearly that my adversary had set himself on the wrong track. If an object lies in the east, and a man has set out westward in its pursuit, no matter how ingenious, cunning, or persistent he may be, he will never overtake his quarry, unless he reverse his course.

I know well enough that a man's character need not be uniformly good or evil, but that some elements of either quality may dwell side by side in his heart. Yet this in no way proves that Good and Evil are fused in one. We can and must distinguish them in every case. And in every case they are always waging a battle—one against the other—in this fierce and beautiful world of ours.

Suppose there is a piebald horse: its coat is composed of different colors, such as black and white. Does this mean that the concept "piebald" negates the independent existence of "black" and "white"? Of course not. The two are simply combined in the coloring of a particular animal. And the same is true of "good" and "evil." Though they may become intertwined and even confused, they could never coalesce into a uniform, indivisible principle.

The letter contains certain other cunning and convoluted ideas, remarkable not so much for their insight, but for their peculiar paradoxical quality.

In the mind's ardent struggle for Truth, there is no room for artifice or ornament. It is a fierce and cruel battle, fought with naked, unadorned reason. Beauty has no part in it. It only distracts us from the truth, and is essentially antithetical to it: a beautiful, but foolish man; a beautiful, but unfaithful wife; beautiful lies … Again and again we are vanquished by falsehoods cloaked in the robes of beauty. Again and again elegantly turned but false ideas—like reckless pilots—lead us into error.

P. 8, *Gottfried Benn*: "Hegel, Darwin, Nietzsche—these were the true cause of countless deaths. Words are more criminal than murder, and ideas wreak their vengeance on heroes and masses alike."

———

April 2

I am like a hunter that pursued his quarry deep inside the steppe, until he finally lost his way. What must I do? I can't figure it out. I can't sleep. I feel trapped. My predicament has plunged me into deep melancholy.

In the morning I wake up exhausted; my ears are ringing. This cannot go on. I am crushed, deflated. I am ready to surrender … Surrender to whom?

This drawn out battle of wits is simply too much for me. Finally I can bear it no longer—I must write a response.

My undiscovered companion! [The address is the same as in his letters to me.] *I hope you will excuse my delay in responding to your initial letters. The fact of the matter is that the questions you raise are long familiar to me. Moreover, I have already resolved them for myself some time ago. For this reason, I did not think a debate could serve us much purpose. I hope you will forgive me: I simply couldn't see any reason to argue, when my own opinions have already set firmly in place—especially when we seemed to be in agreement on many of the points.*

After some time, however, I discovered that this is not entirely the case. Many of your basic premises are fundamentally different from mine. Certainly, that in itself is no great matter: in a world populated by several billion people it would really be naïve to expect everyone to think and act alike. At the same time, I cannot stand by idly while my deepest convictions are twisted and trampled on. And so, I have decided to compose a response.

Life is a struggle. Excuse the triviality. In the earliest times, mankind took part in this struggle on a purely physical, bodily level, alongside other living organisms. Later we invented all manner of arms and set to destroying one another far more successfully, and on a far greater scale. In our own times, physical contest has been superseded by the battle of minds: this battle now rages throughout the whole of the earth, in every land and precinct. And it is the deadliest battle of all. Its outcome will determine whether humanity will keep its goodness or submit itself to the spirit of evil. If evil wins we shall witness an era of absolute moral collapse—at that point there is no salvation for anyone.

This is the war—a localized, one-on-one version of it—that you have declared on me, my "undiscovered companion!" And I have no other choice but to accept the challenge.

Now let us move on to specifics. You propose I ought to believe in Evil in the same way that I believe in Good. A clever move, to be sure: you have confuted mere recognition with faith. The fact of the matter is—my esteemed colleague—I acknowledge the existence of Evil, but I believe in Good. Faith is a preference, a choice. It is a spiritual union with that which we consider a supreme good. Dostoyevsky said: "Where there is no faith there is no good." What sort of thing is it, then, this faith in Evil, which you demand of me? What are you after? Would you have me turn into a devotee of Evil? Shall I yearn for its triumph over Good, and not vice versa?

You insist that I ought not label this or that thing "good" or "evil"— shall I then refuse to distinguish between these two qualities? But if a man has not learned to distinguish one from the other, what difference is there between him and an animal? Shall we not say that the very idea of Humanism is born out of man's ability to distinguish Good from Evil? That the laws of Humanism are grounded in this knowledge?

Throughout the ages, across continents, Humanism has been the guiding principle of all relations between men, my esteemed colleague! Without this fundamental law neither man nor society could survive for a single moment. Naturally, there are those among us that violate this law, openly and with impunity—but we must praise Allah that this world is still sustained by righteous men.

Further, I do not find your philosophy of death especially convincing. If we are speaking of natural death, which comes to man at the end of his life—a life bestowed on him as a gift from God—then I will counter that humanity has long resigned itself to this "evil."

There are other kinds of death, of course—death that cuts life down in mid-flight, robs us of our lovers and friends, surrenders innocent men and women into the hands of villains and maniacs. To please a bloody tyrant and his murderous coterie, death piles up countless bodies in the mass graves of history. How could this panoply of unjust deaths square with your apologia of Death, which has but a single end in view: to cast in doubt the very principle of Goodness, and finally to destroy this principle.

Your ideas on Falsehood ring equally false. To be sure, at certain times men lived amidst lies, and survived by means of deception. I suppose there is no shortage of such people even today. Does this prove that deception is a virtue? No! It only proves that at its very core society is grounded in lies. A just society, grounded in truth, would not abide your Lady Lie for very long, nor would she dare to speak so blithely and haughtily as you presume.

At the close of your last letter you recounted the heart-wrenching story of a woman who killed herself because she had supposedly deceived a virtuous and loving husband. Meanwhile, he turned out to

*have been no angel—and so the poor woman became a victim of her
own delusions, since she believed in the existence of spiritual purity.*

*I think this story is a bit of clever sophistry—a kind of dirty mind
trick. We can cite any number of cases where a wife's betrayal ended
instead with the desperate husband's suicide. Therefore, the claim that
a misguided faith in spiritual purity—which has no basis in reality—is
at the root of all our troubles, seems to me entirely baseless.*

*It would be a mistake to think that the powers of good and the pow-
ers of evil are equally matched, and that so long as we maintain this
equilibrium everything will be alright. Not at all! When it comes to
Good and Evil there could never be a balance, because Good is quite
limited in its means. A wise man had said: "There are many ways of
doing Evil, but there is only one way of not doing Evil—and that is
to abstain from doing Evil." That is all. We must work to do Good,
whereas Evil will be done all by itself, with little help on our part.*

*Finally, I should say that I have very little interest in proving any-
thing to anyone. Everything that I have set out above comes merely
by way of response in a polemic that has been literally forced upon
me. I find your manner of looking at the world deeply troubling, even
offensive. I find it difficult even to engage in a simple exchange of ideas
with someone like you, and I certainly have no intention of making
your acquaintance. Therefore, I advise you to seek out a new, more
suitable intellectual partner, and to leave me in peace.*

Stranger.

April 7

This morning I awoke with a vague sense of alarm, as though I had forgotten
something very important, missed a plane or a train … The first thing I saw
as I lifted my head from the pillow was a letter that someone had left on the
nightstand. My heart sank. Terror shot through my body like an electric shock;
toxic fumes rose up within my wasted soul. With trembling hands I took up
the folded sheets. I wanted only to check the handwriting—of course, it was the
same as always. As I read, however, it seemed to me that besides terror I was
also experiencing genuine curiosity.

*Most esteemed stranger! I hope you know how grateful I am to have
your answer at last. Once more, I am persuaded that my interlocutor is
a man of deeply humanist convictions.*

At the same time, our life may be compared to a boundless marketplace, where each could find whatever he might require. And it is this need that dictates his wishes and desires. Have you ever bought something absolutely useless or unnecessary? And this is my main point: I think you will agree with me that whoever would like to see long-standing canons and opinions continue unchanged and unchallenged will have little interest in novelty. But will you also agree that no progress or evolution may take place without innovation?

If we consider the full history of human civilization, might we suppose that man has ever lived in perfect happiness? At every turn this history is marked by endless wars, famine, terrible epidemics, natural disasters, poverty and violence. In our own times these have been supplemented with man-made disasters: the pollution of water, soil, and air.

Let us leave aside these generalities and examine the fate of a particular human being—you and I, for example: are we entirely happy? For my part, I could not make this claim in good conscience. How could I possibly be happy, when so much violence and injustice is perpetrated all about me, while I am powerless to resist it? My personal feelings aside, how long must we persist in our blind faith in goodness and justice, while everywhere our faith is confronted with harsh reality and shattered in every encounter. Yet we hold fast to our old, irrational conviction, like a blind man that grasps at whatever happens to fall into his hands. Perhaps we too are blind—afflicted with a kind of spiritual blindness …

We must have faith, and so we believed in the mystic powers of water and fire. Over the course of our long history we have worshipped every possible natural phenomenon. And how many gods have we had? And prophets? And great leaders and orators? We had faith in all. What have we gained by it? Have we managed to improve man's miserable lot?

The humanists exhort us to believe in the triumph of Goodness. How long will they lead us by the nose? This triumph has not come, and it will never come. When, in what century, will we finally celebrate this inevitable victory? My guess is—never. And shall I tell you something, friend? Some wishes simply will not come true, no matter how earnestly we might wish them.

Someone might reasonably ask: why couldn't it come true one day? The answer is: because in the realm of reason, humanity has long since lost its way. Our temples of Good and Evil were built with utter ignorance of the basic rules of building. We have no choice but to raze them to the ground and start afresh—i.e. forge new concepts of humanity, conscience, justice, etc.

As Nietzsche once remarked: "The great epochs of our life come when we gain the courage to rechristen our evil as what is best in us."

The stereotypes of days gone by, of habit and received opinion, blind us to the truth.

History has recorded many names whose owners were at one time persecuted, burned at the stake or hanged by the neck, humiliated and exiled—only to be recognized as giants and visionaries in subsequent generations. Some have even joined the ranks of saints. In some of the most advanced societies, countless works of art and literature have been denounced as amoral and destructive—only to be subsequently proclaimed the greatest achievements of human culture. And all of it stems from the fact that we are held captive by our prejudices and our conservatism. Whenever we have the courage to liberate ourselves from these masters, we find the world about us illumined by a flash of higher reason, and a clear horizon of a new life opens up before us.

Our consciousness is in sore need of liberation. We must have spiritual freedom, and it cannot tolerate any obstacle to be placed in its path. Only limitless spiritual freedom can deliver mankind to perfect happiness!

Respectfully,

Your undiscovered colleague.

I could no longer reason calmly. My nerves were like strings that had been wound much too tightly and were ready to snap. I sensed the approach of another collapse. Unable to restrain myself, I rushed out into the corridor, shouting:

"For devil's sake! Who has let this man into my room? What right does he have …"

Hearing my shouts, a nurse came running down the corridor.

"What are you, deaf and blind?" I shouted at her rudely. "What do they pay you to do around here? Who is this man? How dare you let strangers enter my room without my permission?"

The nurse tried her best to console me. She asked me what had happened. But I was far too agitated to give a coherent account of my predicament. All I could do was brandish the pages of the letter before her face. "There! You see? What further proof do you need after this?" Finally, it seemed she was beginning to make some sense of the situation.

"No one came into your room while I was on duty," she said, looking at me strangely.

"How is that possible? Of course someone was here! Where do you suppose this came from?" I shouted, still shaking my letter.

"Very well," said the nurse, apparently trying to make peace. "First, you must calm down. You need to rest. Afterwards, we will get to the bottom of this."

She led me back to my room and gave me a pill.

"Today I think you should skip your morning walk," she advised. "If you are still feeling agitated by evening, please ask the doctor on duty to give you a shot before bed. Does this sound reasonable?"

"Forgive me," I said in a much calmer voice, and I pressed the nurse's hand gently. "I was upset, and I shouted at you. But you must believe me—all of this is really happening to me. I am not raving. I feel like a hunted animal. For some time now I have been receiving letters from a stranger. He taunts me, but he never shows his face. Here, this is his most recent letter. I have been trying to confront him all this time, but each time he manages to slip away. I am going absolutely mad …"

My words seemed to have an effect on her. She gave me a searching look, and for a moment she was silent.

"When did you find this letter?" she said at last.

"Just now, a few minutes ago."

"A few minutes?" she nearly cried out in astonishment. "Well, I haven't worked here very long … I haven't figured everything out yet … But please be assured that I take your complaint very seriously. Meanwhile, you ought to lie down and rest," she concluded, and turned to leave.

The door closed behind her quietly and firmly. I stayed in bed, as directed, but I could not rest. At about eleven o'clock I went to my therapy session, but neither the pert lips nor the pearly teeth of the young doctor—nor, finally, her hypnotic incantations or the soothing music—could pull me out from the pit of dejection.

When evening came I was already drafting my response.

Most esteemed stranger! You and I have been playing games for a long time now. We have been holding a debate, though we have never met. And we have jumped around from place to place, with little rhyme or reason. We have piled everything we can muster into a single pile—all for the sole purpose of proving one another wrong. Unless we define some parameters for our discussion, and determine certain rules of engagement, we run a grave risk of needlessly dragging out this debate for the remainder of our lives.

Now, you have asserted that all along mankind has strayed from the true path, because its guiding principles were nothing more than a tragic delusion; that our ideas about good and evil, love and hatred, honor and ignominy were all distorted from the very start, that our priorities had been picked arbitrarily.

Must we then reject our lofty ideals and spiritual aspirations? Naturally, you avoid speaking plainly, and you would not use a word like "reject"—and yet this is precisely what you have in mind.

But do you imagine that men are miserable in this world because they have observed so assiduously their moral laws? Or is it because they have so often violated them? Are they miserable because their sanctuaries were built on shaky ground, or because we have defiled these sanctuaries or have not kept them sufficiently pure?

Every living creature on this earth strives for freedom, and man is no exception—no one would contest that. But in your estimation freedom is the absence of all constraint. Do whatever you please—no one has any right to restrain you. But what of empathy and charity, what of honesty and conscience—are these not worthy constraints to keep us within the bounds of moral law? You would like to persuade me that freedom cannot tolerate limitations—even if these are the limitations of honor and human dignity. It turns out that actions that fall outside all boundaries—all manner of lawlessness, fraud, prostitution, robbery, etc.—that these are nothing more than manifestations of boundless freedom. According to this logic certain Roman rulers like Nero, Caligula and others—the vilest, cruelest, most murderous, most depraved and most treacherous creatures—are in fact the very paragons of human freedom. These men knew no moral boundaries: cohabitating with their mothers, dragging their favorite horses into the senate, and so forth. But there is a saying: each dog his master, each wolf his god. In the end, justice always triumphs. All who have crossed the boundaries of what is permitted will eventually stand before the judgment of History.

It was perhaps religion that saved mankind from ruinous depravity and a complete moral collapse. And if it has not succeeded entirely in vanquishing the Iblis, the demon of temptation—that demon, at any rate, has been thoroughly exposed and discredited. It was fear of God that distinguished man from animal—wouldn't you agree? It was Sharia law that forbade men from copulating with their own daughters, and not the law of boundless, unbridled freedom and moral relativism.

But if we follow your logic—if we abstract freedom from real life and worship it as an idol, it may be that we will soon return to a state of frenzied bacchanalia.

Shut up in the dungeons of our subconscious, condemned by moral law, all the base concupiscence, the animal insatiability of vice, all cruelty and villainy, ingratitude and treachery—all this evil host clamors for its freedom and only awaits the hour when our resolve should waver and our vigilance slacken. And if this should ever happen—oh, what terrible monsters, serial killers, and brigands will we let loose from the prison-houses of our soul!

Seeing a beautiful woman in the street, you may feel the temptation of lust. We are no angels, after all. But you will not give yourself free rein. Perhaps she is a faithful wife of a virtuous and upstanding man, like yourself, the mother of beautiful children, like your own. This image of the woman is simply incommensurable with your lustful appetite. Here is where you must show your resolve, you must say: "Stop right there!"—because freedom consists of our ability to do whatever we like, so long as it causes no harm to others. But if you cannot control yourself, you will soon find yourself a slave of your own animal instincts.

When the great Socrates was asked: "What is the difference between you and a king?" he replied: "A king is slave to his passions, while I am their master." Yes, Socrates is a hundred times more free than the slave-kings.

The meaning and the substance of life are made up of simple truths. Our trouble is that we are insensible to this simplicity. Willfully, we pick the most tortuous paths, upon which we intend to commit all manner of heroic deeds and overcome innumerable obstacles. Take this example: everyone knows that smoking is harmful. More people have died of lung cancer than of any other cause—I do not mean here the "natural" cause of old age, but the "secondary" causes that stem from our own folly, our vices and various unfortunate habits. Great national resources are expended in the fight against cancer; a global industry has grown up around this disease. Meanwhile, the problem is elementary. Smoking is harmful and dangerous—stop smoking! If you smoke, don't. But no! This basic problem, which could be resolved with only a little willpower, becomes enemy No. 1 for all of humanity. Is it not monstrous? Before our astonished eyes, a tiny speck is transformed into the Beast of the Apocalypse. ("The ignorance of simple truths has been the cause of man's greatest suffering"—there is some Nietzsche for you.) Meanwhile—considering your ideas about man's freedom of choice—you probably imagine that the problem would be solved if we passed a law making smoking compulsory for all. Man must renounce all effort to eradicate bad habits, because that impinges on the freedom of smokers. But this policy will have only one effect: man will remain a wretched slave of his desires.

Freedom is internal; it is our conscience. You may proffer all kinds of "external" freedoms, but if I am a scoundrel and a sycophant these freedoms are useless to me, because I am fundamentally a branded slave with clipped ears—and I will stay this way for the rest of my days.

"What is freedom? A clear conscience." Periander of Corinth said that—a sage who lived some seven centuries before Christ.

Well put, wouldn't you agree? It means that freedom may only be attained by way of spiritual refinement. This is the freedom that we must praise and worship.

You ask me—sarcastically, of course—in what century shall we see the triumph of Goodness? It would be foolish and naïve to imagine that such an outcome would mean the end of Evil. The triumph of Goodness is already here, wherever men have been persuaded of the need to do Good, consistently and indefinitely.

We must be clear about the meaning of victory and defeat in this continuous and endless struggle. We haven't yet touched on this point. A common view equates victory with something like a boxer's blow that sends his opponent into a knockout, or the lightning draw in a Western shootout. In each case whoever ends up on the receiving end is thought to be the loser. What shall we say, then, about the defeat of Jesus Christ—killed by his enemies with unspeakable cruelty—which turned out to be one of mankind's greatest triumphs? In this life there are "defeats" that are worth more than any victory.

What could be more noble than the act of the sparrow, which throws itself into the serpent's gaping maw in order to spare the young cowering in her nest? Wouldn't you say that its death is a great triumph? That it deserves the highest admiration?

What is "heroism"? What is "bravery"? Surely cruel, murderous men ought not be thought brave, nor their willingness to shed another's blood lauded as heroic! Remember Abai's indignant words: "Why are the malefactors praised for their audacity?" Is it really so? And if it is, what shall we say of those who are truly capable of sacrifice? The most fearsome lion is incapable of the sparrow's sacrifice; it lacks the courage to confront a far mightier enemy, to face certain death. True heroism means having the courage and the strength to attempt something that lies far beyond one's abilities.

You argue from the position that the ideals of goodness are incompatible with human weakness, with the simple fact there is no perfection in this world. On this point we are in agreement—but I believe that our imperfections are the engines of our spiritual growth. And without continual growth, life would not be possible. Anything achieving absolute perfection would immediately drop out of the endless chain of evolution and cold no longer continue to exist. Though an artist may strive for perfection in his art, he understands full well that such perfection is actually unattainable. And yet, it is by striving toward this perfection that artists are able to create their masterpieces. Only in its struggle to cure the most dreaded diseases, in laying siege to the most impregnable fortresses, in setting the highest, most unattainable goals, could humanity hope to expand the horizons of its possibilities.

Consequently, the discrepancy between our highest ideals and the reality of human existence is hardly a liability: it is our greatest advantage.

The Almighty has endowed man with a kind heart, good inclinations, and excellent conditions for living, so that we may better the world around us as we grow. But we did not make good use of these gifts. Moreover, instead of searching for the seeds of our errors in our own sinful fickleness, we would destroy all that was wrought by man's soul and conscience—we would deny the achievements of human spirit.

The laws of human existence were written by man himself, and it is up to us to follow them. Certainly, the laws of nature are much harsher than human laws, and many of them run counter to our noble feelings and sacred precepts of morality. But that hardly means that being of nature we ought to live according to the laws of beastly existence.

These laws can tell us nothing about such moral norms as self-sacrifice in the name of God or Love. There is nothing in them about the yearning for a spiritual cleansing through suffering. Only man, and no other creature on this earth, possesses the notion of sanctity. And if so, how could you possibly claim that the laws of nature supersede those of man, and that they alone contain truth, while our God-given morality has no other end in view but to define, expose, and underscore our hopelessly corrupt nature? Shall we, therefore, renounce our moral principles and submit ourselves to animal instincts—and in this way justify all of our evil inclinations? Shall we hold all morality suspect, because there is no perfect creature in the world that can craft perfect moral laws?

Suppose we forge a wholly new system of values: whatever was considered evil will now be good. Murder is perfectly acceptable, because it is consistent with the laws of nature.

A boundless freedom opens up before us! Everything is permitted. All moral shackles have been cast off. Debauch, duplicity, violence, fraud, and deceit—nothing is off-limits, because all of these fall within man's natural rights. One is like a brigand sprung from prison into freedom: steal, rape, and murder all you like! (I suppose this would be something like the "blue-bird" of happiness that you describe so eloquently in your letter.)

No! And a thousand times no, my secret companion! The great laws of this Life were not written by you and I. And it is the weak who break these laws, not the strong. It is the weak who find them too restrictive, not the strong.

Incidentally, the great heroes, burned at the stake and hanged as heretics, the righteous men and the prophets—these were condemned to death not by the people, but by rulers. The people, on the other hand, preserved these martyrs' names from oblivion and have kept them safe in their memory for all time.

Farewell!

Having finished my letter, and hidden it in the secret place, I returned to my room. For a long time I could not sleep.

I remembered the stranger's first letter, in which he spoke of *Yin* and *Yang*, the key concepts of ancient Chinese philosophy. I could accept the interpermeability of these two opposing concepts and constituents of the whole. But why should these two principles coalesce and become something uniform and indistinguishable? Why should they lose their distinct and independent meanings? Why should white be mixed with black, the useful with the harmful, the good with the wicked? Unless we gave ourselves over to rank sophistry, we could not reasonably equate the fire that burns in the hearth with the destructive flames that mercilessly consume a man's home with all his livelihood inside. And yet the basic mechanisms of burning are the same in both cases. These are two very different phenomena, even if both may be reduced to the same basic principle. What can we possibly gain by refusing to distinguish them?

The ones who stand to gain from such ideas may be regarded as moral degenerates, the hermaphrodites of the soul, slippery amphibians that can see nothing wrong in serving the two masters: truth and falsehood. Yes, these degenerates are forever scheming against the world: they would love to revenge themselves upon the rest of us for their grotesque deformities.

And I can tell that my "undiscovered companion" has something of this quality. Like some terrorist, he is hatching a plot to blow up the spiritual temple of humanity—the temple that was built through the moral efforts of countless millions. He would like to see destroyed and negated the results of millennia of human effort. He would have us revert to a beastly existence, where moral goodness has no place.

We must fight against moral terrorism with everything we have.

The Hound's Death

(*excerpt*)

By Muhtar Magauin

Just before dawn, when the sky had barely begun to lighten in the east, he and his master rose and set out on their journey. The snow that fell in the night had been swept by the winds into lowlands, and now its white patches stood out against the dark crust that covered the steppe as far as the eye could see. The valley looked busy and brooding, as though quilted together from dirty scraps. In the pre-dawn hour the air felt stiff and sharp, like a steel blade. Like a stream, shackled in ice on a windy day, the steppe lay in ponderous silence among its squat boulders and jagged ridges, and there was not a living thing in sight, save for a few sparse patches of dropwort brush. Whether it was from the cold or the excitement of a possible kill, a shiver had been running through Lashyn's body from the moment they left the house.

The *auil* lay behind them. After a short time the hound's step recovered its usual spring and confidence. He ran about a lasso's throw ahead of his master, dodging now left, now right, scouring the underbrush for tracks of potential prey. Kazy knew that chasing down a fox would be no easy task on a day like this, but he was nevertheless optimistic. Maybe fate would smile on him, and chance would grease his saddle straps …

The sun rose above the horizon, dividing it from a long ribbon of cloud. It was large and round like the lid of a cauldron, and red like iron when it is held over a fire. Its rays shot out in every direction, but seemed only to add to the cold. And yet the world around them was transformed. The petrified steppe heaved a sigh and came to life. Although the shade side of the snow-covered peaks still looked dark and menacing, the sunny side now shimmered with pink and golden sparkles, while the shallows where the fresh snow had gathered turned into pools of pure silver. A short while later, when the gloomy, long shadows grew shorter and lighter—as though melted by the climbing sun—a hare darted out into a clearing far ahead of them. Lashyn's paws had been throbbing with impatience all morning, and though the hare, sensing danger, immediately dashed up the hillside, the hound set off in pursuit. In no time he was closing the distance between him and the hare. Racing behind, Kazy could already picture the red blood dashed against the white of the snow as he cut the hare's throat, and its lifeless body hanging from his saddle. Lashyn must have imagined something similar … But their hopes were frustrated. The hare, hearing the crunch of snow growing ever louder, flew like an arrow. Lashyn ran as fast as he could, but the distance between them refused to shrink. They came out onto a plateau: although the snow here had been packed by the wind, it was still too loose to hold up a grown dog. Lashyn could see that the hare was getting away, slowly but surely …

He had chased down many foxes and hares in his time, and he had learned a thing or two about them. He knew that some were slow runners, not made to sprint, and there were others that flew like the wind. There was more to it than just getting close to the prey before it could spot you. But this long-legged snow hare, who had already started to molt—the tail was noticeably darker than the rest of the pelage—was a different story altogether. One moment he was wound up in a ball and the next he was stretched out in mid-air—and he raced so fast that no living creature could ever catch up to him. But Lashyn had never been outrun, and he was far too proud to acknowledge defeat. Never! Sooner or later he would catch up to the hare, take hold of it, rip it to pieces … He tried to run at an even pace, and the blood of innumerable ancestors coursed gladly through his veins—all he had to do was keep his eyes on the hare.

Climb after climb, drop after drop … Lashyn's legs felt as though they were made of lead, but he refused to give up the chase. Finally, when they crossed a valley overgrown with *kiyak* and blanketed with fresh snow, and began another climb, Lashyn noticed that the hare was only a lasso's throw ahead. Its pace was not as frenzied as before, and its long ears drooped from fatigue … The hound gathered all his remaining strength and made a final push. But the hare—fighting desperately for its life—was first to come up to the ridge, and from there he dashed down the slope, toward a thick growth of pea tree bushes. Worn out by the chase, Lashyn just clacked his fangs as he watched the hare vanish into the thicket.

Frozen branches whipped at the hound's face as he tore his way trough the bramble. The hare had gotten away. The dense pea tree brush, hugging the hillside as far as the eye could see, was shot through with hare trails—twisting, looping, merging, and branching off, so that it was impossible to stay on track. Gasping for air, Lashyn tried one set of tracks, then another, then—realizing that he had lost his quarry—he turned back.

Kazy, the skirts of his coat flapping fiercely at his sides, was galloping toward him, and when he saw the hound emerge from the brush he jumped from his saddle. He carefully examined the dog—going over his face, his fangs, the heaving chest—but saw no traces of blood on his white coat. Could it be …? He was even more surprised than disappointed. Until then, Kazy had supposed that there wasn't a creature in this world that could outrun his hound. Perhaps the trouble was with the thin ice-crust that had covered the snow and now gave way easily beneath a dog's tread …

The hare-hunting season had already passed, but this was nevertheless an unfavorable omen: if a man riding out to hunt should meet a hare along the way, he must chase it down. Otherwise the day's hunt would not be successful, and the next day might be no better. But there was nothing to be done about it now. Kazy examined the hound's paws—they seemed sound, but the dog was sluggish, and his eyes looked out in embarrassment. His body, covered in prickly frost, trembled slightly. Kazy took off his coat, made from teg pelts, laid it down on the snow, and wrapped it round his dog. He produced a small piece of yellow sheep lard from his pocket and gave it to Lashyn.

When about as much time as one needs to milk a sheep had passed, Kazy mounted his horse and turned back toward the *auil*. There was nothing to be done—it had been an unlucky day, and he had simply to accept it … But Lashyn evidently thought otherwise. His strength had returned, he even seemed well-rested. In his usual manner, the hound ran well ahead of his master, scouring the underbrush for animal tracks—albeit with little success.

In this way they went on for a long time, until they reached a broad plateau. This was grazing ground. The ice crust was everywhere pierced by sheep's hooves. Here and there, flaky snow, mixed with earth and ice chips, cradled small piles of fragrant, dusky dung. A few sparse patches of dry grass, trembling in the wind, were all that had survived the migrations of countless flocks.

Lashyn, who had nearly given up hope of reversing his fortunes, quickly picked up an unfamiliar scent. The scent was fresh—it seemed the animal had come through here only a short while ago. Lashyn spun around, sniffing the earth, and spotted a set of the tracks. They were ordinary dog tracks, stamped in the snow amid a sea of hoof prints … But the scent … No, it was certainly not a hare. Not a fox. The print was too large. It was an enemy. Definitely an enemy … All at once, Lashyn felt a surge of excitement. A shiver ran through his body—from the very tips of his ears to the tip of his tale—and the hairs of his coat stood on end. For a moment or two he stood still, as though trying to calm himself, and then he was off.

Lashyn was certain that his enemy—whoever he was—had followed the flock, which had scattered out over the grazing ground. The hound trotted softly, careful not to lose sight of the tracks. Climbing up to the ridge, he saw below him the patched quilt of the flock—black and white sheep fanned out all along the hillside. Small clusters of them had gathered about dropwort bushes and dark thaw-patches. A *shopan*, squatting on the opposite hillside, was piling up pebbles into small *korgans* to pass the time. Below, at the foot of the hill, his hobbled horse picked at the wilted grasses left over from the previous year …

All of a sudden Lashyn saw a large gray dog that he had never seen before. The stranger moved about cautiously, pausing now and again behind some mound or ledge, as though hiding … The hound felt his heart beating wildly, and he let out a piercing, furious cry, shattering the frigid silence about them. He yelped again and again—this was unlike him—and all at once flew down the hillside like a cannonball. Far behind him, he heard Kazy's cries, cheering him on.

Sensing danger, the gray froze for an instant, then turned sharply and ran toward the tall, rocky hills. He was troubled not only by the human that now pursued him on horseback, but also by the large, broad-chested dog—he looked back at Lashyn again and again, inadvertently slowing his pace. The hound caught up with him just at the very first ridge.

His master's voice egged him on, and Lashyn—sensing his opponent's fear—lunged at the perineum, as he would normally do with a fox. He wanted to lift his prey off its feet and whip it against the hard ground, but the gray turned out to be much heavier than Lashyn expected. He had a hard, muscular body, and Lashyn could see now that getting on top of him would be no easy matter. He had barely flinched when Lashyn's teeth sank into his flesh.

At the same moment, sharp fangs clacked just above Lashyn's ear. The gray had twisted his head backward and tried to take hold of Lashyn's snout—he barely missed. His eyes swelled with blood, he made another lunge, flashing a set of long white fangs, and once again Lashyn was able to dodge the attack. The gray caught empty air, but he also succeeded in breaking free from the hound's iron grip.

Lashyn heard a cry—it was Kazy, galloping toward them. The gray took off once more, leaving behind a bloody track. Lashyn raced after him, furious that he had been unable to wrestle him to the ground. But he saw clearly enough that this was a powerful opponent, and also that he had come out unhurt thanks only to his lightning dodges. At the same time, he felt no fear—on the contrary, his fury redoubled his strength and courage.

After the time when he nearly killed Bardasok, Lashyn had gotten a taste for fighting. *Shopans*, passing through the *auil* on their way home from wintering grounds, feared to let their dogs loose on his account. Quick, nimble, and powerful, like the best of his breed, Lashyn lorded it over the guard dogs that were often his equals in strength. Though now and again he too got a taste of their fangs, the hound always came out on top, while most of his opponents never dared to set foot in his *auil* again.

Thinking back to his old triumphs, Lashyn decided to try an old strategy: all he had to do was wait for the right moment and then grab hold of the wolf just below the ear or by the throat. The wolf, in turn, saw that he could not outrun

It would heal. The other wounds—on his chest and shoulders—were mere scratches. There would be no trace of them in just a few days. Kazy was glad to see that blood had stopped gushing from the larger wound.

He was right—within a few days Lashyn had virtually recovered. His flank wound—the size of a human palm—festered for some time, but finally it too closed up …

Kazy, on the other hand, had caught a chill in the frigid wind, and took to bed not long after they returned.

The fresh snow, fallen the night before, was pocked with countless tracks. Everything is as clear as day to Lashyn: who went by, where they were heading, how long had it been … Over there a yellow weasel hopped through on three legs. Its tracks disappear under a dropwort bush and reappear again in the open snow … It is as though all of it is happening right in front of him—just over there the weasel darted off to the right. But Lashyn is not interested in chasing such a small animal … This set of tracks, coming from the opposite end—that's a ferret. A ferret is also small, but it is agile and strong, and audacious. His master loved ferrets. Sometimes, when tracking a fox, they would spot a ferret—and they always went after it. But today Lashyn was in a hurry. Maybe some other day, when his master returned, they would have a chance to go after a ferret … A fox's tracks. Looks like she came through here at a brisk trot, playfully waving her bushy tail. There was no reason to run after her. Here is a little fox cub—let him prance along, no harm there. Another fox. The tracks are fresh—he must have been here only a few moments ago. You could tell by the prints that it was a male. Now he is dashing through the snow somewhere, glimmering in the sun like a living flame … But he must be somewhere near, just over that hill or the next. Ah, pity!

No, he couldn't hold out. No sooner had he climbed the nearest ridge, keeping cautiously behind a ledge, than he spotted the fox, wandering about in the pea tree brush in the valley just below him.

In the next instant Lashyn was already racing toward his prey, cutting across the shallow hillside. By the time the fox could sense the approaching menace, Lashyn was within a lasso's throw. The fox did not get far before Lashyn had him pinned to the ground.

But here was something new: the thrill of the chase was virtually gone. Why did he run after the fox? Why did he catch it—for whom? What was the point of killing the animal? He couldn't say. The fox was splayed out motionless before him. A drop of blood dripped from its snout onto the snow. The hound looked about him—was someone there? No. No one. How could it be? Wasn't his master somewhere nearby …? Lashyn, remembering now why he left his house, left

in his life tasted fox meat, he felt regret at the memory of leaving it behind in the snow.

All about him, within a radius of two or three steps, the snow was encrusted with blood. Lifting himself off the ground, Lashyn set about licking his own congealed blood.

His hunger had abated, at least for the moment, and the hound felt the strength slowly returning to his body. He understood that he could not free himself from the iron jaws—only his master could do that. And he would help, if only Lashyn could reach him. If only he could …

The cast-iron wheel, chained to the trap as a weight, proved impossibly heavy. Each step cost Lashyn a tremendous effort. The broken bones at his elbow rubbed one against the other and made a crackling sound. It would have been easier if the forearm caught in the trap were taken clean off—but it refused to part with the rest of the body and hung on by muscle and sinew. With each step, when Lashyn leaned on his right arm, red and green flashes swirled before him, then dissolved in a gray fog.

Nevertheless, inch by inch, he made steady progress. Sometimes the iron weight got caught on a rock or a bush. At such moments it seemed to Lashyn that he would never move forward another step. But each time, after a tremendous struggle, he managed to break free. Once the weight got stuck between two trunks and refused to budge. While he is here, fighting a futile battle, imagines Lashyn, a cauldron, laden with meat, is bubbling on the stove back home … At last he managed to drag the wheel back, guide it around the trees, and drag himself out to clear ground, where there were no bushes or rocks.

Still, the trap grew heavier with every step. No matter how smooth his path seemed, there were always unexpected obstacles, hidden beneath the snow. The most difficult task of all was to climb to the top of the mound where his master was laid. In the past Lashyn could make the short climb in just a few bounds—but now it had turned into a steep mountain. Luckily, by that time his injured leg had frozen entirely. It merely hung there—strange and lifeless, but no longer painful. Gathering all of his remaining strength, the hound crawled forward. The sun had nearly touched the ground by the time he reached the top of the hill …

Lashyn howled. He howled for a long time, his howls broken only by plaintive sobs. What else could he do but howl and weep when the most terrifying of secrets had been revealed to him …? Man, the master of all living things on this earth—he that breathed life into dull, insensate metal, transforming it into a swift-footed steed or a soaring eagle according to his desire—man, the almighty and all-merciful, also dies! Like the little lamb or the field mouse! That was why his master had stayed on this hill for so many nights and so many days. And there was none in this world that could help Lashyn, bleeding from his wounds, whose strength was ebbing away and who was living his last hours on this earth … Lashyn howled, lamenting his master. He howled, sensing his own approaching death. He howled, parting with this earthly life, with the great expanse of the earth and the sky …

Death came quicker than he might have expected. A hungry she-wolf and her three pups, who had been prowling about the wintering grounds for some time, devouring the scents of human life and the rich food, heard the miserable howls and straightaway set out to investigate. Lashyn's cries proved an ideal beacon. Coming near, the she-wolf quickly surmised that they had come upon a solitary dog that had wandered out into the steppe, and that no humans were nearby. Fearing that this stroke of luck might be spoiled if the dog tried to flee, the wolves took care to surround the mound on four sides, and only then—with their eyes blazing and their long white fangs gleaming—they charged at their victim.

That day Lashyn had suffered so much—a secret so terrible had been revealed to him and robbed him of all hope—that he was no longer capable of feeling terror and astonishment. His life no longer held any meaning for him. And yet he was still alive, and life has its own laws.

And so the hound did not surrender to his assailants, did not bend his neck to receive death's final mortal blow. The wolves had counted on an easy prey, but the hound was able to repel their initial attack—only the she-wolf managed to land a blow on his hip. The hound's fangs flashed with lightning speed, keeping the pups from coming close enough for a strike. The wolves retreated, but in the next moment they launched another attack, with redoubled strength.

Lashyn was alone, and his attackers were four. He was hobbled by the trap, but they were free to maneuver about him as they pleased, searching for a way in. The scales were tipped against him. The she-wolf, who had seen many fierce battles in her life, was certain that in no time she would lap warm blood and fill her belly with fresh meat. In her impatience she had become careless. All five were tangled into a wheezing, clacking ball, roiling in a cloud of snow dust. Lashyn was pinned down at the bottom of the heap—but just as the wolves were about to tear him to pieces, he made a lightning strike and ripped open the she-wolf's belly.

The cubs did not notice their mother—convulsing in the snow, trying desperately to take hold of her own innards—until they had finished with the hound and his bones had been picked clean. The dog proved too scant, too emaciated to fill their starving bellies—it had only whetted their appetites. Seeing the blood gushing form the terrible wound, they leapt upon the she-wolf.

After only a short time, the only things that remained of her, who had borne and suckled them, who had raised them to be strong and merciless, were a tip of the tail and four rough, frozen paws.

Poetry

Earth, Hail Man

By Olzhas Suleimenov

...

A riddle:
Why do men reach for the stars?
Why does the eagle soar
in our native songs?
Why anything beautiful
made by the human hand
we have called lofty?
Rivers nourish the fields,
cities rise up on riverbanks,
and the Earth like a heart bursts forth,
gripped by its watery veins.
It's not easy—blazing a trail
to the dim stars of the day before last.
But the earthly path is harder still—
the path you had borne in your heart,
the river that circled the earth,
that welded city to city,
the light that raged in the void
and ignited the fire of your youth.
Not a command—
a commandment:
find the path, the map
that you followed to reach the stars.
The path of the earth—an extension
of the road you took
to the blazing stars of today ...

I

Old heavens singed
               by the April dawn. Good.
The clouds—good.
I just like the look of them.
Suddenly you remember
the bottomless void—of the universe.
And a shudder clips your broad smile.
That's just me:
in an airplane, flying high,
engines humming along,
everything is just fine—
you are humming a little tune, I see—
go ahead—it's relaxing, I know.
And there isn't much else to do
to keep you from dozing off.
Suddenly,
there is an announcement,
you must climb out of your seat—
a few more bars would be nice—
the airplane pitches its iron jaws
and swings to the right.
Through the bulging eye of the hatch
you make out the signal fires.
The engines seem to be sputtering out
a secret, menacing code,
and the hump on your back
is stuffed with flimsy thread.
It is a moment of catastrophic inflation—
all of a sudden everything is unbearably precious:
the cushioned ease of a tattered sofa,
the flickering kitchen lamp,
the moment when memory resurrects
everything lost,
the full futility
               of the ticked-off years—
a moment can burn like a flame.
Days forgotten
and years blanked,
time moves through the subtle spaces of trepidation:
every one of you will carry away
the blow of fear

the flash of joy,
no matter what strict regulations apply.
You step to the hatch.
You stand at the edge
of a fearsome, bottomless night—
pierced by signal stars
burning somewhere miles away
on an invisible earth.
Impatience mutters behind you—
"Permission to pass my turn …"
Granted.
Step aside, then—
I will be first
to swallow up the abyss!
Borne by the rumble,
seared by the night—
gravity my only direction—
I soar …
my body dividing the void,
and the world tumbles up to me.
Pop—the parachute mushrooms
somewhere far over my head,
delicate straps shoot up into the skies.
Silence.
Not a body around!
I am roaring with laughter,
shouting!
I am not afraid
of crashing!
I know now
that Earth is beneath me—
full of earthly miracles!
I have dampened her ardor
with a parachute,
in the night
with the tip of my boot
I found her.
In a meadow I sank …
Man over Earth!
Freed from the tyrant gravity.
My dear man,
I know what it's like,

I know
that a new age dawns at moments of
                        great trepidation!
The first age began, my dear man,
when the primordial ape
tore its palms from the sod
and raised to his astonished eyes
two rough, impossibly heavy hands.
That was victory.
You are the one that tore
man's destiny
from his dear, green planet,
lighting over it the dark flame
of cosmic mystery.
So it began—
                the Second Great Age.

… A smile,
a wave of the hand—
like a signal flag
        raised
at the starting line—
a deep breath
                of the brisk April air.
An instant!
And all the air has shrunk
to a tiny blue ball.
Earth—on a monitor!
Earth—on a monitor!
Wreathed in smoke
or stardust.
A couple of folks
on the sidelines,
nobody said a word.
Then somebody stirred:
"Maybe too soon …"
Yes, comrade,
I know,
        I am worried too—
for him and for Valia,
for anyone bound to this life,
and whose duty it is

over the depths of the sea—
Earth, bow down before Man.
Here is your god—
I am.

The first age is prehistory,
the age of laying down roads,
the age of splendid swords
never sheathed,
of sovereign orders' defeat,
of radiant verses' triumph.
A faceted meteorite,
launched from a sling,
flings an eagle's velocity
into the skies
like an arrow.
Wind whipping cloaks
over sweat-drenched rumps.
Fire! And Feathers!
Earth tumbling up to the eagle,
steeds pounding the sod
at the speed of death,
where they fall
the final battle will be fought.
Speed,
cast in bowed, serrated steel,
fells all in a swing
that must fall.
All that must pour out its agony
in the smoldering grass.
The steeds will fly over you
wailing their dirge.
All that dies—dies with a thunderclap,
like an atmospheric discharge,
all—
          that means you,
my broad-backed ancestor.
Festive skies tempt
your prehistoric eye,
disheveled stars cast down
a menacing eye,
moons look down

if the battle is won!
The radio operator
half-mad
pounding out
screaming dashes
        and rattling dots
                into the terrible air! …
Cliff faces, furrowed by time, recede;
the stormy eyes of the sea
look down
on the foam-white trace.

… What have I seen of the past—
besides the stately halls
                of natural history,
docile daggers gathering dust
in glass tombs.
Golden epaulets side by side
                with embroidered gowns,
ploughshares, amber rosaries,
        fibulas, all that dreary etcetera.
Plates of worn asphalt underfoot,
like a permanent *takyr*,
the lawns exhaling
a tepid fragrance
of living flesh.
Entry is free
into a forgotten, unfathomable world.
Getting out—that was a good deal harder.
Everything was just as it always had been,
larger than life,
the years rumbling by,
in that deafening roar of time
we strove to tear free
for good
of centuries past,
we ran,
our days flickering
like suns in our eyes.
The calendar changed
half a century ago,
a full century behind

that is why I long
for the soulless, bottomless skies,
every instant dying to break
                through the silence.
I will leave all behind—
grasses, gravestones
on the flat earth below.
Ah,
but I'd love to take to the skies with me
a fiery steed!
Speed! More speed!—
that swallows the road.
A man on the road,
speeding forth,
will hear the drone of his blood.
A galloping man
wants to lift up his wings
and fly, with an eagle's smile
smeared on his face,
roaring with laughter
over the abyss,
and believe in the colors below,
in the plunge,
and—in the radiance of the spring skies.
We have created ourselves
through the sum of all suffering
down the ages;
we will press our lips to regions
before us unknown.
The light of the earth,
like my memory,
flying beside me—
only the most audacious designs
are discernible
from this impossible height.
I would tip my wing
                to the land of my birth,
like I did so many times before—
but the capsule is not made with wings …

with a tip of their wing?
There are thousands of paths
in the April sky—
but Gagarin's points straight up,
like a granite peak
shooting up suddenly
in the hilly steppes.
No eagle can reach the top,
but the boldest will solemnly
circle its might.
Love.
He is loved. He is sure of it.
He is calm.
Someone's heart aches for him.
Chosen, one out of thousands:
loved—meaning worthy.
The morale officer was asking about Valia.
Mother—
           that's what we call our steppes,
Sweetheart—
           we call our steeds,
everything that is dear to us
is called by your name,
woman.
Woman—motherland,
woman—history,
the artist has painted the woman Liberty,
grass, meadow, even weather—
all feminine,
sky is half-woman,
my courage—entirely.
This is probably why
women stand
by the beds of men.
Even the howling blizzard,
the sinking sorrow
are women.[3]
Life, it is you I love,
because you are a lover true.
… Cliff faces, furrowed by time, recede;

---

3   The allusion here and above is to the original nouns' grammatical gender. The
    Russian *sky* is neuter, *courage* is feminine. [tr.]

the blue of the ocean eyes
looks down on the foam-white trace.
So eagles break from the earth
and never look back.
I am tracking you
from the Kazakh steppes,
as you fly all alone, among
the invisible stars.
There is none in this world
who did not take notice
of your ascent.
You gave all:
your daughters' dowry—pride,
a burning heart—to your wife,
to me—a terrestrial poet's
inspiration.
Courage was all you carried aboard,
honor, an atlas of starry roads.
From above
            the terrestrial sphere
is a tangle of roadways
yellow and blue,
and red.
Mountain ranges
and piney canopies
lie farther below.
He went up to see
where the roadways end,
to look at the rectangles,
at the curvature
and Cuba,
drifting slowly toward the east.
To see the flares of uprisings,
the pentagonality
            of the desert, the green,
                        the crimson soil,
to listen to history,
and of course
to hear news of his distant homeland:
"White helmets in Leopoldville …
Man shot in the Atlas peaks …
Cape Town falling down on the pavement …

A young pioneer retreat near Alatau …
Blacks, Indians, Arabs singing,
marching,
clutching the butts of their rifles …
The walls of the White House
are splattered with dirt …
Black flags flying
over ancient Hellas …"
Hey kid,
how does it look from up there,
under the spotlights of ageless stars?
Tell us,
will Guinea be free one day?
Will the cities of Second Century
be as fearsome as those of today?
The First Age!
Today we are tallying the score
of all that was seen and done.
The Vostok went up
on the shoulders of laboring giants.
There it stands,
There it flies—over everything perfectly ordinary,
over our past,
so it was;
it marched like a parade
over the rippling oceans,
saw it all:
the lore of glimmering stars,
the sheen of gasoline rainbows.
These blue screens have a tendency
to hold on to whatever their tributaries
haul in from the land:
gold,
granite, crushed by the jaws of time,
kilowatts
of untapped, undiscovered energy.
… To calculate the velocity
of a dream in flight
men learned to count billions.
Swords had been swinging
for many trillions of seconds;
legions marched over this earth

the age of seeking.
Remember how frightening
                              seeking can be.
The cinders of quests for Truth,
the stems of flowers—
are behind you.
On roadways, traced by the stars,
man fashions his gods
and his foes,
and finally arrives at mankind.
What is that path?
That long and unstoppable path,
that life, young and fierce, and ours!
I am asking you, man,
not to forget
that on this day
you are one age older.
World,
          Earth,
                    the terrestrial sphere,
the conjunction of words,
nations, swords,
and destinies—
how many steely hooves
flew over you!
Your deserts are judging us,
who were pitiless.
We, the iron rulers, trampled you,
we, the Khan's horde,
marching to Mesopotamia,
we, mighty warriors,
trod through the steppes,
conversing with you in a fearsome dialect.
We razed Rome,
we destroyed Taraz,[4]
ravished maidens yellow and white,
we looked at the world
through the slits of our eyes,
our hands came together
in combat.

____

4   Taraz—medieval city in Kazakhstan destroyed by Genghis Khan.

the sun
is a heart that beats in the earth.
They believe:
we are made for living.
We too believe
that there is no East,
no West,
there is no boundary to the sky.
There is no East,
no West,
but two sons, born of one father.
There is no East,
no West,
there is sunrise and sunset,
and the magnificent word
EARTH!

Magnificent in every tongue.
There are no Batu Khans,[5]
no Napoleons,
only Einsteins
and Tsiolkovskys.
No divisions—
only millions,
only victories,
and no draws.
Because:
there are places
where dying is an honor,
dying free,
dying for freedom;
there are places
where living is misery;
there are places
called sorrow.
Meaning, new stars
                    are still born,
meaning, sparks still fly.
Meaning, wherever eyes
turn embrasures—

---

5   Batu Khan (c. 1205–1255)—a grandson of Genghis Khan and the ruler of the Golden Horde.

the terrestrial path,
the extension of the trail
to the stars,
conquered
this day.

V

Old heavens singed
       by the April dawn. Good.
The clouds—good.
I just happen to like the look of them.
Just think
      for an hour or two
of eternity …
and you too will long
for the pebble Earth,
for clover and rye …
That's just me:
here I am, in a spaceship.
Pressure—normal.
You are stuttering a little tune
through the radio.
Visibility, clarity—never better.
Time to come home, you say.
That's an order.
Your voice quivering a little.
My dear, dear people—
what a magnificent order!
I won't lie,
tears shed in spaceships
      are never of fear.
I believe!—
dreamers, poets, scientists.
I believe!—
tears and calculations.
At 10 a.m. Moscow time
pitch-black skies
      spread over me.
Devil take you,

sweetly conquered.
I roll in her grass …
I tear off my helmet …
There is a slightly bitter taste
in my mouth.
Hold on, I'll just cut
the parachute straps,
I'll look for that flower
in a tangle of grasses.
Don't I know you from somewhere?
My sweet, native land,
we rush through this life
never noticing
that our earthly meadows
marshal great armies
of long-lost *Ivan-chais*6
to greet us.
Maybe that Ivan
had also gone
to the ends of the earth,
and returning to native shore
he stood,
      swaying,
he fell in the grass,
his hard fist clutching
the stem
of his namesake flower.

Earth,
you have kept for me
the brightest of days,
a white kerchief,
dashing
past the slender trunks
of the birches:
—What … who are you?
—Son of the Soviet land.
Tell them to come.
—I will! Were you flying?

____

6   Ivan-chai (lit. Ivan's tea)—Russian folk name for the willowherb (gen. Epilobium).
    [tr.]

wrote.
Sleepy pilots and airmen
                        are tossed in the air
by admiring crowds.
Today—
on the twelfth of April,
all the poets,
            impervious to the charms
of the little buds on the birches,
are snapping their lines
and pencils.

… Radio paints a portrait:
"Broad-shouldered"
I straighten my shoulders …
"Young … round face …
Twenty-seven …"
The same age!
Not that it matters …
"Graduated from an industrial college
                    with perfect marks …"
I did a stint at one of those!
"Lived on River St."
Mine was *Aryk*!
"Honest, forthright …"
Well, I'm not much of a liar …
"Loves reading and operettas …"
Me too, a little less of the latter …
"Doesn't smoke …"
I suppose
I'd better cut down.
I usually play center back,
but I can also do forward.
I don't mind falling—
I don't even notice the pain.
I'm generally good at math,
well-versed in astronomy,
basically,
            I'm a walking encyclopedia—
and I teach at the night school:
anything they want to know,
and I happen to be broad-shouldered,

… At a workers' assembly,
an old man, white as snow,
stood up and said quietly,
"We're proud of you,
Yuri Gaganov …"
A small error,
but no one corrected him.
No—
he was right,
a letter or two
doesn't make any difference.
What matters—
is that his flight took off
                    from a Soviet launch pad.
What matters—
is that peaceful men walked behind him.
What matters—
is that all of us
                    are equal
before his triumph.
What matters—
is that all the nations of the world
                              sincerely
shook our hand.
"Who are you?
Where are you from?"
said the captain quietly.
He knew better than anyone
what oceans can do to men—
like the ocean that raged
all around them.
Ziganshin spoke for them all,
"We are Soviet people!"
We are born in late autumn,
warmed by the searing speed
                    of our distant journey,
tried by ice,
by the sword
and the ash.
We were first to drain the full cup
of sorrows

Words Spoken Over A Cradle

By Mukagali Makataev

The reign of peace on this earth
is like to a child's sleep
in the nursery hush.
Though you have woken,
let your child sleep a while longer.

Sleep, my son, my little one,
unmindful of kings' treasures
and their wars.
But all that I have won,
all I have stored up and treasured
will be yours.

Your wondrous smiles
are a father's greatest joy.
You prattle with a mystic tongue
that tickles my heart.
What mother's child
does not return again and again
to those years of childhood hush—
the years of a child's
sweet and joyous calm?

The reign of peace on this earth
is like to a child's sleep
in the nursery hush.
Though you have woken,

whoever you may be,
let my child sleep a while longer.

The Sentinel

When you send greetings to Murat,
be sure to end with "Peace to all the living."
"What news? All quiet?"—
just those few words and nothing more.

You have known the frosts of winter,
the nights and the long pre-dawn hours.
You have known this life—a life that keeps on living—
so long as all is quiet.

These days only the scars remind us of the war—
and the fire that still burns in the old men's hearts.
Their children died in the name of peace,
but their line is not extinguished.
Our old man is like a mighty poplar—
soon he'll be going on his second century.
"All quiet?"—is his first question,
whenever he sees a familiar face,

be it old or young, brushing past him.
"All quiet?" he whispers to each in turn.
And when a storm is brewing, he looks skyward
and says calmly: "All quiet up there?"

Life is still much too fragile, and so
our old man stands watch night and day.
Should he close his eyes, even for an instant,
his grandchildren would vanish in the void.

Live Until Sixty

You've seen it all,
grown used to it all,
you've taken much on faith,
and given all.
Now you've reached sixty.

My father would have lived so long,
had he not died in battle. So it goes.
He'd be wandering still
his native streets, a little grayer.
But so it goes.

War—whoever dreamt you up,
you, enemy of earth and sky?
If not for trenches and crossfire,
he would be off to work this morning,
enjoying the warm weather
and chatting with his grandson
in the park—the poor old man—
or trying to make heads or tails of my poems.

I never let the fields lie fallow,
I didn't leave my mother unburied
or my son uncared for,
and I've never killed a man.

So, you've reached sixty—
seen it all,
given it all …
I wouldn't mind getting that old …

I just love the wondrous, ordinary old men ...

I just love the wondrous, ordinary old men!
There is nothing they don't know—
these fathers' sons and grandsons …
Their numbers are dwindling, it seems.

What words of wisdom have you left,
you shards of antiquity,
what have you still tucked away
in custom's satchel?
What riches more will you dole out to me,
to pass on to future generations?
Bring them forth, and I will be
a worthy heir to your treasures.

I will keep the vows given by my elders,
I will honor their teachings.
I will thirst and hunger …
for I too will be called to answer.
Our lives are growing more difficult with every day.
Soon the old men will leave us altogether.
Though I could not bend like a bow,
I can be firm, like a suit of armor …

The Trail

There is a trail that runs near my house—
but finding it is no easy task.
It is lost in the wilderness—
memory's meandering trail.

Down that trail my father went off to war,
and it leads to my grandmother's grave,
and a child had wandered here before his time …
I've set a marker down for each one.

"So many ditches lie hidden by the roadside—
and it's easy to lose one's way in the mountains,"
so spoke my mother, as she led me down the trail.
Those creases on her face—those forking paths …

I trip and I fall up and down that trail,
and I never tire of looking for the path.
There are so many wondrous trails—
I trip and I fall … and I keep walking along.
I'm dead tired, why pretend?

After Work

Why don't you bring me some *naswar*, old man.
Day in, day out—it just drags me down.
Maybe I'll run away some place …

Old man, you say you knew my father?
Tell me, was he as reckless as me?
As hopeless a smoker as me?
As come-and-go as me?

Like me, a useless prankster?
Did he set men's hearts on fire,
like those that sow the seeds
of doubt and revolt?

Did he look anything
like his son and heir?
Our elders used to say:
"Tell the father by son's arrows."

Old man, you say you saw my father
when he was beaten down?
He looked to you?
You gave him words of courage?
No crying now, old man,
or I too will cry.
He rose and quickly went his way,
just like my father.

Youth

What did I get from youth?
(What is youth's use?)
A lesson in revolt,
a life-giving flame,
and a blazing sword.

It cast the chains
that bind me to my art,
it sent me scrambling up the barren cliffs,
it forged and tempered me,
showed me the meaning
of a life well lived.

It did not pass in vain—
it blossoms in my garden still.
Youth gave me sight and reason …
I haven't let it go …

A Lovers' Dialog

"What if one day I vanish from sight, like a bird?"
"I will spend an eternity looking for you?"
"What if I burn to a crisp from fright?"
"Then my ashes will be mixed with yours."
"And if I come back as a heavenly mirage?"
"I will be the wind that cradles you."
"And if I bring you nothing but cares?"
"Even that wouldn't turn my heart."

Should I Write Verses?

I can't say whether I should write or weep.
Who is that standing before me?
A wayward dream, it seems …
Must I console it or strike up a dirge …?

A wayward soul sways before me
like a wisp of gray smoke—
a withered sapling,
robbed of its tender fruit.

"These days I can't remember you …
can't find you."
"Forgive me, I've come to see you
one last time …

"Though my fruit are still unripe,
the fire of my youth is extinguished …

There was a time you dreamt of me.
Remember me, forgive me,
for our sake …"

Yes, I remember now—
there was a girl … (long lost from sight).
A *tandyr* stands now
where she used to stand.

Nothing remains now of her youthful glory,
except the eyes, perhaps,
and the pitch-black hair.
(My love had crumpled me like a soiled page
and tossed me in the fire.)

Yes, I remember our meetings and our partings,
your daydreaming
through my long-winded declarations,
your betrayals …

You had given me a dream
and vanished—
I searched for you along the mountain passes,
until I finally lost my way.

I raced after you, kicking up dust …
I had become a withered grass blade.
But I remember everything …

I threw open the doors—
I let my dreams go free
and never said good-bye.

Still, let me keep this one dream.
O youth, my youth, I never understood
your lesson, and now I cannot say—
should I weep or write verses?

My heart brims with buried treasure ...

My heart brims with buried treasure.
All evening long
I've walked these alleys,
lined with lovers' benches.
I remember now …

We sat in this same garden—
it must have been autumn or summer,
so many years ago—
sat on a lonely bench
and warmed each other's burning bodies.

Just then we heard a shadow's steps,
and as it passed
I thought I heard a mutter:
"… unmindful of the dawn …"

My Thirty-Fifth Spring

Thirty-five.
Thirty-fifth spring.
Thirty-five.
I've seen it all,
scorched by thirty-five summers,
thirty-five winters
toiling in the earth—
it's no small change, thirty-five.

Will I see thirty-five more?
I remember my father,
bent over his desk,
straining to read the history of the
Communist party.

I remember a day in February—
father holding up his draft notice …
I remember it all—
the churned-up fields, the village, the school,
the teachers and the hard bread
of the schoolhouse.

I just can't seem to remember
moments of joy and sorrow …

I was a farmer's son,
walking behind the ox
since I was ten.
I had traded some bread
for a bullet,
and sent it to my father
at the front.

I remember my grandmother—
so quiet, so serene.
I remember the samovar's flue—
how mournfully it sang
when a wind rose up.

But I can't remember
if I had been a clever child.
No one praised me for it,
at any rate.
I just remember that one day
victory burst into our village
like a bird, a week late.

So I grew—
a soldier's burning flame,
still burning …
They look at me and tell me—

Once it was a humble man's abode,
and though he toiled night and day,
all of it came to naught.
All his life, he thought himself a slave
(with a single change of clothes to his name).
But a child was born to him—a first-born son—
an answer to his many long prayers.

A coarse hemp cloth was laid out for the *toy*—
(and there was nothing to serve over it).
And this was how my grandmother received me
from the womb of life.

Later my father became a leader of his people
(and threw away his old rags).
There, by the side of the ridge,
stands a ruined crypt.
My life had its beginning there …

February 1941

The snowdrifts of 1941
swept in
and dressed the *auil*
all in white.
A wind had risen
from the gaping abyss of war,
groaning over earth and sky.

Rise up!
Day after day war sends its notice,
bidding men trade in their shovels
for arms, day after day
it comes as a fearsome enemy
to do battle.

The moon, old horseshoe, hangs
on a flimsy nail.

one that will never leave for warmer climes.

My love, do not be cross with me—
and do not ask me for all-consuming passion.
I offer deep respect and understanding,
since lately I've felt myself extinguished.

You

So, you've got a bit of sense,
              a touch of wisdom,
and you believe in mankind …
You are like builders' cranes—
you can lift up
and set down.
Time's current runs within you—
between your open palms,
              down along your spine …
You say to your little ones:
"We'll take the flames too,
              we'll feed the fire."
You are the tinder of the age,
              and its ash can.
You burn,
       brushing the ashes from your bones.
You are the lock that locks the secret coffers,
              and the key.
Young *jigit* that trod the paths of glory,
              returning as old men—
except those that vanished with no trace
in fierce and bloody battles.
You are the treasures hoarded by your fathers—
you that thundered from your earliest days.
You ran like rivers to the sea,
poured out like grain upon the earth.
Mightier than your ancestors,
tougher, more steadfast than camels,
you are your children's native soil.

The Curse of Korkut

(*excerpt of a verse drama*)

By Iran-Gaiyp

*Set in the times of the prophet Rasul (Muhammad), at the turn of the 8th c.,
near Syr-Daria*

Prologue

(… heavens … earth … a deafening silence … the Great Silence …)

TUMBLEWEED

(disrupting the silence)

I roll through the world—
I! …
I! …
I! …
I! …
All through the universe
there is none weightier
and more solid
than I! …
I am like to a God! …
I *am* a God! …
I am a God! …
I! …
I! …
I! …

THE VOICE OF THE WIND

(driving the Tumbleweed)

… and I—I am the Wind …
Whatever
there is
I can knock down,
crush,
drag
wherever I wish! …

(howling)

Oo-oo-oo! …
Oo-oo-oo! …
Oo-oo-oo! …
Oo-oo-oo! …
I am a God! …
I am a God! …

VOICES

No, *I* am! …
I am a God! …
I! …

(a struggle between heaven and earth)
I! …
I! …
I! …

(Enter Korkut)

PART ONE

(... the dome of the heavens ... the great steppe ... in the midst of the steppe stands Korkut ...)

KORKUT

(addressing the Heavens)

Neither by day, nor by night
do I find peace ...
Nature,
my mother!
My fortress!
Poetry—
life's nectar! ...
Without them I am nothing.
And what of all the rest?
O Tengri!
Men despise me ...
I wish to compass the whole
of the world,
to comprehend it,
but they mock me,
they jeer at me:
Fool ...
Lunatic ...
A peddler
of useless trifles ...
O Tengri, why—
why have you made me so?
I know that nothing is done
under the heavens
save by your will ...
But tell me this:
Was *I* also your will,
or a moment's whim?
Answer me,
O Artificer,
do not delay! ...
Three years,
three long years,
I dwelled in my mother's womb ...
Remember?!

Three whole years!
Tell me why
I alone
had to wait all that time,
when a human child
remains in the womb
but nine months
and nine days ...
By your grace
I came into the world
a stranger,
a monster ...
All of creation
was then in revolt! ...
The Sun and Moon
flew off their orbits,
and the heavens
were covered over
with black clouds.
And the seas surged forth—
no patch of dry land
could be found on Earth.
All was under the sea.
Was it not so,
was it not so—
because *I*
had come into the world?!
And was it not I
who sowed fear into the hearts of men
long before I was born?
All—
fell to the ground before me ...
Their knees buckled
from fright ...
In their hearts
men called me
Korkut!
Korkut—
in other words
Terror!
Terror!
What else could I do then?

No one knows—
no one could ever know
what I am—
what sort of thing I am.
Only you,
my Maker,
my Tengri,
you alone know my heart
through and through.
You know
that I do not live
but *tarry*
on this earth,
in this human form …
My flesh is ashes and dust,
while my intellect—
as if it were made to mock me—
has grown mighty …
Why did you grant me wisdom,
when I cannot bring to life
the least of what I know,
of what I desire …
I—
an eagle with clipped wings,
barred from heavens,
doomed to tread this earth
in boredom and madness—
Why,
answer me,
why have you made me
so,
Tengri?

(he pauses—no answer comes)

I could tell many things
to men,
but there are none
that will listen,
none that could understand,
O my Maker.
My courage and my will

are strong,
but my spirit
is poor.
I am meek and guileless—
because of my faith
in You.
But there is a fire
that courses through my veins—
a searing passion
to give sight to those
who were born blind—
O Tengri!
I would wrench open those eyes …
Then the people would see
the Path in the darkness
and rush forward! …
But I am powerless—
no one
is in any hurry to see …
they only know
to sleepwalk in place,
to recoil
like frightened sheep,
to bellow like the mad …
until pacified at last
they resume their empty,
meaningless chatter …
They bleat:
We're doing just fine
without this Tengri …
What's He got to do with us?
They shout at the top of their lungs:
God is Buddah!
Or—
God is Ieshu-Mashiah,
meaning the prophet Jesus,
whose fate was sealed
by a Roman Prefect
with well-washed hands …
There is only one God—
only You!
only You!

But could any created thing
be God?
Yet, at this Kagan's court
the gods are multiplied without end:
there are gods all down the hierarchy—
the merchant and the sycophant,
all the human chaff
that grovels all day long
before the throne ...
Convulsing gods!
Divine contortionists!
Their swarming masses
have blotted out the sun—
they are everywhere ...
O Maker,
how much longer
must we suffer them?!
(*Nothing ... Tengri is silent*)

A single word!
Have mercy!
Lift from me—
if only for a moment—
my dark sorrow ...
Won't you tell me
why all that was white
has turned blacker than night?
Or can it be
that you are the greatest lie
of all?!
What, silent still?!
Silent ...
Won't you give me
some word or sign?
Or is your silent answer
sign enough—
a sign that never more
shall I have peace
or mercy ...
a sign that this life
is worthless ...
Then hear this:

O Tengri!
Not a soul …
So—then we two
must die together.
Collapse … Confusion … Death …
But if I must die
a dog's death
I shall curse You
with my dying breath!
Will you abide this!?
Have you turned
into stone?
The firmament is pitch black—
              no flash, no spark comes …
That pitiless heart
will let no tear drop,
no sigh come forth …
Know this, O Petrifactus,
from this moment on
I will not serve You.
Forget all that my heart
had confessed to a Stone,
and set me free.
I am bound to forget you,
O Tengri!
From now on,
I stand alone
in the unfathomable universe.
Alone—
I, my own God!
Al … Dunya …

*(… a solar eclipse … a terrible rumbling … the earth quakes … a cliff that had
stood nearby crashes down to earth …)*

CLIFF

Now you've gone too far!
Open your eyes!
Have you forgotten, Korkut,
that pride is a sin?
The higher you soar

CLIFF

You have offended Tengri.
You have dug
your own grave!

KORKUT

I dug it?

CLIFF

Yes, you alone.

KORKUT

Will you instruct me, then—
you rot and ruin,
a heap of gravel
by the roadside …

CLIFF

Fool!
You think yourself eternal?
There is an end to all,
you too will be brought down.
We raise ourselves up
only to fall down,
you also will see death.

KORKUT

I will not be cowed—
will not recant
my words.
From now on
I am my only God!

(… *peals of thunder … lightning bolts streak the skies … one of them strikes a
Shyrgai-tree and it falls to the ground …*)

O wonder!
What sound is this?

(listens)

It is quiet now,
but no sooner had the metal
pierced its bark
the Tree—
sang out!
It sings!
It sings!
And its mournful voice
cuts deep into my heart,
this rich and plaintive sound …
It fills the whole of this wasteland,
the firmament,
all that is in the world
swells
with that wondrous sound!
It is my heart that moans there,
my soul
that cries out!

Meditations at Medeu

By Fariza Ongarsynova

I

One used to prancing in the saddle
will often stumble on the ground.
This is no walk, no gallop—
a swirling, streaming carousel,
where none may turn to look behind.
And I am drunk with the beauty
of soaring mountains,
of shimmering cliffs!
A frigid beauty.
Icy silence.
The sun bursts forth—
it is within arm's reach,
as though a painted picture.
All mirrors, mirrors—and beyond.
All spinning, spinning—
joy and terror—
go, go,
don't fall behind.
So the eternal law:
this life is but a wondrous rink—
one false move
will knock you off your feet—
where all are racing
on strips of senseless metal,
thick as a serpent's tongue.
All's fair, I suppose—

speed demands a leap
of faith.
This life
is but a wondrous rink.
There is nothing to hold on to
and none will take your hand
of those that ply the icy trade
step by step, and lap by lap.
Yes, life is a wondrous rink.
And Medeu—a stiff whistle-blow,
alloy of ice and sun,
and the blue of the sky,
the gasp of contest—
and the race that is over in a flash.

II

Yes, life
is a wondrous rink,
so long as your footing is sure …
I am cautious,
timid.
I hear a whisper at my back:
"Don't trip …
You are too lovely—
don't trip, don't fall."
But life had other plans.
Icy tears
roll down my cheeks.
I am here again,
beneath the stars of Alatau,
where once we lived,
and hoped to live forever.
I hear the icy whisper
at my back …
I had climbed to the very edge
of the cliff,
and the wind cradled my brow.
"Oh, won't you rescue me!"
I pleaded.
I am chilled to the very soul.

My arms stretched out
toward the abyss,
I cursed my helplessness.
I did not recognize your smile
when you came
to push me over the edge.
Love passed like a fairy-tale.
You used to call me
a bird of the steppes,
a rare steppe flower …
Now my love is a prisoner
of your blind memory.
My life,
a trusting child,
cried out to you:
"Have mercy!"
But a fickle heart
is a merciless judge,
fate is a willful mistress.
And so, I have stepped out again
onto the blinding ice—
so softly, timidly …
I am a cautious sprinter,
I still remember
the madness of the race.
And you that did not help me up.

III

So lofty and so free … I shudder,
my head is spinning.
The mountains teach with beauty,
and freedom is what they teach.
Alatau—my native home.
I race along the icy expanse—
blue,
glimmering,
blinding.
I swallow summer's ardor,
I am drunk with silence—

there is not a sweeter taste.
Life—
a wondrous rink.
I am flying,
and you could not.
I race along the icy expanse,
past envious, adoring eyes.
Life—
a wondrous rink.
I am a sliver
of Alatau,
of my native mountains.
Why didn't I slip sooner
from the icy grip?
But the avalanche sweeps me up
and carries me along.
And it seems to me
that I am flying into heavens
with a mountain peak
perched in my palms.

Visions of Northern Palmyra

Column, capital, caryatid—
words that came so late …
This chapter of glimmering dusk
is finished, my head droops …
It strikes! Again!
The clock-hand stands at two.
A starless night—like a spear
frozen mid-flight
blazes over the earth;
the night is a meteor,
burning over my head,
lighting the path homeward
for my wearied thoughts.

My humble, desolate home—
it too stands awake,
yearning for rivers,
for pools of water in the sand,
seared by my betrayal
on a sultry night.

The two of us—we used to dream of water.
That much is true.
For many years visions of Northern Palmyra
swayed before us, like a mirage
on a hot summer day—
there, where the steppe is bursting
into blossom,
where it races like a steed.

O blazing city—a marvel of precision,
a harmony of water, skies, and buildings.
The Neva—a giant vessel carved in stone—
streams oil into the smokeless lamp,
and rolls the clouds along,
adorned with stately masts.

I dreamt of the desert, saddled with stone bridges,
in the leaden canals I saw reflected
my native earth, scorched dales
with their wild horses.
With hooves cracked on cobblestones
they came to drink
from northern waters.

Four rearing Scythian horses
found me here, a fugitive:
this was the city of my dreams—
the river waters blazing
with scarlet skies,
and houses of stone and marble
rose up and swayed over the barren steppe.

My thoughts, soaring over Neva waters,
assume true classical forms.

This vision of the city
is the muses' harmonious chorus.
What treasure shall I carry home?
What shall I give you?
I clench a fist of summer heat.

Intervene!

By Zharaskan Abdrashev, translated by Ilya Bernshtein

P oets are quiet?! Not so!
    With the force of a manifesto
They say what they mean!
I place at the head of these poems
One verb:
                "Intervene!"
I know
That this is my duty,
                my aim,
                        my right.
To intervene in all and in everything
Is no mere delight:
It is an obligation.
You have been obligated by
Your country and all other nations,
By the timid moon in the sky,
By the irrepressible dawn:
Intervene—do not wait,
And your word will find echoes.
Against villainy shut the gate
With conscience and honor.
Let that voice not die
Which summons to noble action.
To intervene in big affairs is your duty,
Your duty is to intervene in great affairs.
There are no trifles here.
Remember that in all times

Poets have felt no fear,
Going forward despite
Authorities on feet of clay.
Valor is your civic duty.
Therefore, do not delay!
Linger not at the crossroads!
Intervene in everything in your way,
Dig down to the nitty-gritty!
Squeeze out your inner slave
Drop by drop, but do not become
A little idol of a god.
Rejoice: you are cast by fate
Across all the longitudes
And latitudes of the globe.
Intervene: by night and by day,
At dawn and at sundown.
The world turned upside down
Can use such interventions.
In offices, apartments, public squares,
Try to be everywhere
In the very thick of things.
Let the sweep of your deeds
Declare your omnipresence.
If some do-nothing should ask,
Hiding his smirk at the bottom of his glance,
"Hey, you, what is it you want?
You want more than everyone else?"
Tell him: "Yes!
More than everyone else!"
For to see and to make believe
That your vision is impaired,
To know and all the time
To pretend not to know—
There is no
More unforgivable crime.
May no human trouble of grief
Pass by your eyes or your ears
And not stick in your soul
And shatter your peace forever.
For Happiness, for Good Will among Men,
Intervene in solemn service.
With each letter that flies from your pen,

With each word,
                with each sentence.
Who said that poets are quiet,
That they cannot fight for the truth?
That they remain unseen?!
Not for nothing did I say it:
At the head of my poems
Stands the verb:
                "Intervene!"
Not for the sake of amusement,
Not for the sake of bravado,
But so that the planet might know it,
In all things to intervene,
To intervene is a duty for a poet!

Let's Get Acquainted, Time!

Collecting my spirits, I take the floor …
                                    Thus,
I will talk to you, Time.
By birth I am neither worker nor boss.
I am a citizen of my native Kazakhstan.

Yes, his head was bare, his feet were bare …
But a sharp sword his carpet-bag did puncture.
In nineteen seventeen my father dared
To seize the liberty he wished for.

He was undaunted, terrible he was,
And everywhere the cymbals of Equality did clang
When he, not sparing his strength,
Cut down his foes in battle, with no other aim.

I learned about my father's battle-fame
From rumors and from tales.
Nor later, though he risked more than his name,

In fighting for the truth did he once fail.

Although in faded archival documents
I have never seen my father mentioned
He wore the rank of private with such pride
As if that rank were higher than a medal.

I have inherited my father's proud stance—
Long may his glory endure unsoiled—
Absorbing it into my muscles' strength
And into my heart, where the lava of poems boils
Thus,
I will talk to you, Time.
By birth I am neither worker nor boss.
I am a citizen of my native Kazakhstan.

My Law

My law—
So full of justice and of grandeur!
You seem to me no less than a colossus.
You gave the right to me, who am a Kazakh,
To call himself a Soviet citizen forever.

O Law of mine!
You are my whole life's foundation.
My spirit
That sustains me every second.
You are the light that shines on steppes and mountains,
You are the arduous mountain pass that beckons.

O my Law! My healing spring!
You are the light that lights the road
And the journey.
Allow me now to sing an ode
In praise of you, as many have done before me.

He did not hear the strain of Abay's[1] songs,
In his common-sense ideas he caught no poems.
Whence is the West illumined by the sun
Unless it be from the East's majestic summits?

Broad is the world. But that man knows it not
Who is a stranger to the earth's exaltation.
Otherwise, it would also be his lot
To see that the time-whitened East itself
From the blooming steppe receives illumination.

---

1   Abay (Ibrahim) Qunanbayuli (1845–1904)—Kazakh poet, composer, and philosopher.

Our Battle Cry

There's a country that boils
                    like a river in flood,
There's a country that lives in bright dreams of the future.
To this country alone
                    does the world, like a steed,
Entrust its reins, confident that the rider
Will not turn from the path but continue forward
If he but hears the call of the people:
"Communists, onward!"
Yes, our ways were thorny and steep
But the outcome was guessed long ago.
The Revolution's tempest, terrible and deep,
Would sweep aside in a flood each formidable foe.
That is when this battle cry was born:
"Communists! For freedom—onward!"
How furiously did they then set to work!
Gradually, the country moved forward …
Once again a conflagration flared out in the West.
Nineteen-forty-one of tragic memory!
Once again the battle cry rose up, like ringing bells:
"Communists, onward!"
There's a country that boils

like a river in flood,
There's a country that lives in bright dreams of the future.
To this country alone
                    does those the world, like a steed,
Entrust its reins: for he who preserved it
Will not swerve from the path.
                        And even today
Our battle cry rises above our planet
And even today
        we call in alarm:
"Communists, onward!"

My Autograph

(to a foreign artist)

Who your forefathers were,
        now vanished in time's abyss;
And to whom you were born,
        your mother, your father, by name;
And an altogether difficult question:
        who are you yourself?
And who would you like to become
        over time, in the end?

In each of us our ancestry
        has left a memorable trace.
Our names and patronymics are not
        merely doodles and nothing more.
You must know whose last name
        the poet proudly bears
And what land gave him birth—
        that, too, you must know.

These facts will suffice
        his fate to foreguess,
To marvel and see that his verse
        is not without breadth,

To see if his voice has strength
>or is just empty breath,
And even to picture
>the face on his portrait, more or less.
If all this is so,
>then why should I stand apart?
If all this is so,
then I fear not the days to come!
Here's my new autograph:
>from now on, under each poem
I'll write: Kazakhstan,
>and beside it: USSR.

Man's Worth

Man! Man!
I adjure you, listen to me!
I have one thing to ask and one thing alone:
Fear to become a miser,
Prizing Man above everything else, whatever it be.
Flaunt your happiness not,
>nor your well-to-do home.
What would you do if you—
Listen well to my question, listen well!—
You were left all alone in the world, all alone?
No, no need to deform your mouth with a crooked little smile.
Try to imagine that this is
>by no means a dream.
Above the earth blazes a blinding blue sky
And there's no one around—not even a mouse or a bird
And not even a man, to bring nature to life.
This world, without life, without blood,
>is all yours!
Therefore, reign! ... But reign over what, over whom?
>But no matter!
All is yours—the seas and the woods.
All is yours—the empty villages and cities.

The rivers flow just the same, the mountains still stand where they stood,
And Mt. Everest's snows look just as pretty.
Walk through the gardens—their only gardener is you—
And the fruit will quietly drop in your hand.
Only a trifle is missing—life—the rest is for you
And your wealth is beyond any wealth known to man.
All is yours—airplanes, ships, factories, banks.
How splendid it is to rest your gaze upon gold:
Old coins—dollars,
                    drachmas,
                            and francs.
In your hands the keys to all highways and byways you hold,
All roads and streets—and no people at all anywhere.
Well, have you pictured it?
                    Now what would you like to do?
Will you shudder from a thought, monstrous and strange,
A thought for which you
            are unprepared?
You're a hunted animal with the mark of vengeance on you!
Bang your repentant head against a cobblestone of gold.
And nightmares will fill the silence with terror and fear.
Scared of the beat of your heart, where will you run from your soul?
Man! Man!
I adjure you, listen to me!
I have one thing to ask and one thing alone:
Fear to become a miser,
Prizing Man above everything else, whatever it be.
Flaunt your happiness not,
                    nor your well-to-do home.
What would you do if you—
The question remains the same—
You were left all alone in this world, all alone?
Would you really reach for the moon, crying "Mine!"?
Sticky fear would glue the mask of fear forever to you.
And awake or asleep, you would cherish one dream as your own:
Once again, as before, to catch a glimpse of a friend—
To catch a glimpse of a friend, once again, as before—
And should it turn out to be a glimpse of a foe,
Just the same, toward the foe you would go,
Running,
        laughing with joy,
And kissing your erstwhile foe.

To Abay, or on Comparisons

Father-Abay, the transformed countenance
Of my native steppe is beautiful beyond compare.
Look closely—and you'll see at once
How obsolete the old comparisons are.

What flowers have grown in a steppe of prairie grass!
It has absorbed your children's labor.
In speaking of Almaty, "paradise"
Has long ago become a common label.

Where wit succeeds, the tongue of praise may fail,
May remain, without any reason, helpless.
Listen: Bibigul sings like a nightingale.
But can such a comparison do her justice?

Words heal our souls and yet, nevertheless,
At times they give us no help whatsoever.
Though you might call a Lada a "tulpar,"
It's clear that the comparison's a lame one.

The eyes are too slow for all that is new
And for the beaten path speech searches still.
You can compare a cosmonaut to a falcon but you
Still do this out of habit, without skill.
Father Abay, one thing I'd like to see—
I'd like to see words in their primal splendor.
And to whom would you compare the poet himself?
For the creator of comparisons there's no comparison!

Your radiant greeting—send it to my heart
That I, warmed by your goodness, for my part
May pay you back with love in every poem.
And let all people whom I once held dear
Enter into the crystal of my tear.

Enormous world, you have become my fate.
To make up poems is the only way I see
To express how proud I am of you,
Enormous world, that is bequeathed to me.
So that the days might stay forever blue
To your own self, above all, be you true.

As long as my heart still beats, so long live I
And gaze insatiably upon the earth
And I absorb the blueness of the sky,
Receiving all your beauty in my heart.
And even there where light can never go,
My world, that you exist I yet will know.

A Meeting with the Future

An evening meeting
Between the poet and his readers.
The audience listens.
My meeting
With kindred spirits,
Realists and dreamers.

A meeting with youth,
A meeting with the past,
A meeting with a friend,
Dependable and handsome.
Like a new level,
Like a new height,

A meeting between a grandfather
And a grown-up grandson!

A meeting between the author
And his contemporaries,
A meeting between a tribesman
And his relatives,
A meeting with a poem of eternal youth!
A meeting with reality,
A meeting with truth!

An evening meeting …
A meeting with those who invited you,
Who redeemed your failures, who justified you,
A meeting with critics
Most severe,
A meeting with the foes
Of yesteryear.

An evening meeting …
A decisive meeting!
A meeting that's like a final battle!
You were sure of yourself only yesterday!
An evening meeting
Between you and fate,
An evening meeting
Between you and destiny!

Time of Silence

By Bakhytzhan Kanapianov, translated by Peter Oresick

The divine punched card
will be distributed
according to Descartes' logic,
and the broken line of fate
according to the x- and y-coordinates.

"When the line ..."
Boris Pasternak

When the masters lose the wisdom
they once earned by feeling …
Then the game begins.
It is almost an art.

And the rules of this game
the world grasps at once.
But it doesn't extinguish
their nightly hearth fires.

And the Muse with her pipe, alas,

will not give any heavenly advice …
And still the line of fate
will not reveal the poet's fate.

————————

The wise sun, toward evening, gives me
its sacred image in rays of light.
In every thing it is reflected,
having cut the poetical path.

Then a tiny Viennese street lures me
by the G clef of its being,
and things vanishes in the mist
of the hours of the dying day.

The sun does not pay tribute
to our earthly vanity,
and there is a certain mystery in nature
as it shines behind the night distance.

The Mozer Clock

At the drawing of a breath,
the steady tick of the clock—like a clerk
whose abacus clicks: balance due!—locks
out that which is not timeless.

Somewhere in the world
steel is fired, bread is baked,
and the poet Mistral is caressing
ancient stones by the shore.

Somewhere spawning is driving
a whale, against all good sense,
up the wild river
and turning out the soul.

Somewhere a jet's radar
converts time into space,
travelers knowing this gift
only after their travels.

On this side of the window
the steady tick of the clock in the flat
measures the shoots of the grain
giving birth to thoughts in the world.

The fullness of being
wrecks the rhythms of the heart.
Somewhere a judge passes
sentence upon the dissident.

Again the steady tick
clicks the balance due!
Yet my destiny is to fall asleep
at the drawing of a breath.

This old clock
with the metal spring …
And on the celestial scales
the fate of the earth is balanced.

And who is entrusted with the key
is known, perhaps, only by God.
There, a star turns, its ray falls
to illuminate the road.

A Story

On the outskirts a house
breathes through yellow windows.

Shadows in the window frame—
I know—two are at home.

A mother, her fatherless daughter.
I'll stand at the porch.

Keeping silent, I'll knock
and ask for water.

And I'll be given a drink …
Everything will repeat.

In a few more years
the same light in the same window.
A mother stands on the porch,
a fatherless son is growing up.

———————

The night train,
the trip that wasn't planned.
The match lighting up the dark
showing me the gist of things.

Having traveled through the life zone,
I am forced to disembark.
All roads lead
to the heavenly station.

And Through

Jetstream …
my windshield fogs, and a bird,
chilled by the heavy shower,
is spreading one wing.

Distressingly, the wipers creak
an almost human sigh.
This video clip is out of focus;
this era is in the turbid stream.

I'm just a casual passenger
in it, like the chilly bird, but
we'll be helped by the evening paper
to understand the starry & vapid sky.

————————————

The skyscraper sleeps like a Sphinx
remembering the famous Dakota tenant.

The street in the rain—it is the Styx
on this prayerful Saturday night.

Poets and ghosts
are wading Broadway,
checking the classifieds
under "Muse."

The bird will not meet the bullet
at this musical's finale.

And there from atop that building—
I do not know which storey—
I'll hear the bird singing
and in the song a bid to fly,

and the sound of heels rounding the corner
and the laughter of a beautiful woman
and Brubeck's blues beneath the window
and then the low melody of copper.

————————————

The breathing of my beloved
slightly shook the silence.
Blessed by an angel, maybe,
in the form of a butterfly.

I'm not trying to solve
the mystery of a woman's rest,

but I'll screen moonlight through
through a curtain so as not to fall

upon her head.

————————————

Again the white page,
At night the snow had drifted.
At night your life will change
to a nomad's way of life.

The poetic line will lead you
far from your own arbour.
And endlessly morose, the raven
sits somewhere on the branch.

The Part Played

Your role, so perfectly played,
drains me of speech, of sanity.
And the secret pain of the epoch
sleeps upon your shoulders.

And the bullet will become a bird,
And there is no past anymore.
And now upon the last page
falls the light of the other world.

————————————

The train wheels rumble,
tearing you from the quiet
of the earth. Will it be the lights
and people at the junction
to untie your knot?
Earthly distance is distressing.

The train window effect
in the night steppe
multiplies your reflection
and somewhere sums up the fate
reflected just outside the glass.

A Museum. A Lamp

Inside, the shadows of the past are black.
And in the resonant circle of stones
the secret of fire is kept,
which no one dares to fan.

Heavy with its own weight—
that of a thousand year old fire—
The Iron Age.
The lamp in the form of a horse.

Among the Leaves

I don't know
which bird, but a bird
flexed its wings
making a rustle.

Or maybe
it was the leaves,
the leaves hiding
the bird in the crown

and she,
she doesn't want
this bird to nest
in the leafy crown

and with its wings
from within the leaves,
the leafy prison,
it is waving and waving.

———————————

On a mountain path in the mist,
on a mountain path in the snow
by chance I'll find a line of verse
like some change in my pocket.

And, repeating it, the mountain
river will find a happy couple
at the bridge in a small place
where the river turns off.

The stanza gives birth to the image,
struggling within it like a bird
and all on the mountain
will come out to the path in poetry.

It's like a cloud breathing in the valley
during the autumn bonfires
and like the cold wind at the top
where the eagle spreads its wings.

On the mountain path in the mist,
on the mountain path in the snow,
we're seduced by the world around
that gives birth to the line.

And there's nothing I can do
and there's nothing I want
and I am speechless before it
and I don't light the candle.

I'm simply a stenographer,
and I don't need authorship,
as my way to the heavenly temple
will not be repeated by anyone.

Ostankino

The concrete TV tower—
its majestic spire rising over the city, spreading its wing so far
that somewhere a satellite is plowing the heavenly fields
stretching it, stretching, until the first meeting with a UFO.
My oar is not resting in Ostankino pond.
I plunged it in and I put away my tricks.
And into the reflected spire comes the past day
sparkling in the water, and again Koroleyov's fantasy
pulls me at night towards Zvezdny Boulevard
like a bird, not finding shelter under this sky,
will fly towards the Cosmos Cinema
where the group seance lasts all night,
where at the entrance there works a watchman,
a poet with a broom and part-time astrologer.

Almaty, Kazakhstan

Your name was Alma,
an apple,
I called you
half
of a green city.
Your name
was hurriedly
scribbled
onto the blue page
of the airline ticket
when I was hurrying
to see you.
You were joking
during our meeting,
"Hey, you're translating
my name wrong!
It is 'don't take' in Kazakh,
it is like a forbidden fruit which
you aren't translating
correctly, oh, not correctly."

The Valley

Into the valley dripped the day's image,
the shadows gelling.
The bush by the stump
transformed into antlers.

The night floated behind,
near the pregnant cloud, breathing
through the layer of glass air
over the steep mountain.

I'll enter the night … But
the white horse jumping down
from the burial mound
will drop dew in my palm.

In it will flare up the image
of the day through a crystal ray …
Everything will be repeated
without me in a distant valley.

The Tourist Trip

I scoured Athens
hexameter by hexameter
but didn't find
what I was looking for,
only ruins.
I was late
by hundreds of years.
I settled down quietly
into the coffeehouse's corner
to weep over my ancient ways …
I wish I could find the time
to read *The Odyssey* sometime.

———————

The language I forgot as a child,
the notorious bilingualism,
under which I am losing my own face
and becoming two-faced, give me
to understand the aboriginal,
a stranger to me, who is going off.
But when in the middle of the night
in a dream I kneel before my ancestor,

I realize he doesn't believe
I am a newcomer
from a heavy oppression. He grins
to the side: You are not worthy
as a successor.

Once when I burst out crying in a dream,
a magic word was whispered to me.
In the morning I couldn't remember the word,
and my mother shrugged, "Don't know, son …"
A magic word for dear people
seems like a fish in the net of days.
When I go to sleep in the night silence
again the word comes to me.
And in the morning I can't find it,
can't remember. Only the sigh
which doesn't translate to poetic lines.
And if our son takes someone's burden
from their hands and cries a little
in his dream, having moved it,
will the cherished word pass through?
And if it passes, will he remember?

Not knowing his own pedigree,
not knowing his own clan or kin,
not knowing the principles
of his own language, a child is crying
who isn't yet a year old,
and in his crying is hidden
a depression he can't yet express—
a rude remark or simple request—
it isn't clear.
And all of this he will carry into the future
and cut into truth, into lies.

Autumn hid itself among the treetops,
the leaves rustling.
It doesn't ask for anything,
no words are needed.

Like in the ancient story
where people do not exist.
Only black trees
through the autumn light.

The Song of the Vagabond

I have ten coins,
my grandmother's gold coins.
I'm anxious to see the world,
to put more light in my life.

I'll put my razor in my luggage,
two shirts, a couple of books,
and I'll keep the prayer in my head
the old man used to sing from his balcony.

I'll wander around the world,
I'll take off to see the world,
the price of my ticket
these few gold coins.

My heart is drawn by Paris
where Boulogne Wood doesn't sleep.
I'll witness, in each country, a miracle
out of seven miracles.

I'll walk along the asphalt
throughout foreign lands.

The famous N
will open its S

These coins with a royal profile
I'll scatter along my way.
Perhaps in the young brunette's house
I can find lodging for the night?

And suddenly my hand
may lay down upon her breast
and passionate breathing
may put out the candle.

And all of my wanderings
will help me to reach
the heavenly ladder,
the smiling God.

We don't need light in the dark,
I'll have seen a lot of the world.
A sign of a good life
is a shapely woman's profile.

I'll be sure to clean my razor,
I'll be sure to write a book.
The old man's balcony prayer
will flare up in my memory.

———————

A mountain road in the mist,
where the visibility is dreamlike,
alluring with a mystical power
that compels you.

And somewhere, on some slope
time is turned slightly back
and everything transformed
so radically you're baffled.

The chronicle of my past life
stops running at the bridge,

Somnabulic Sonnet

Where the Patriarch ponds are breathing
by the evening light reflected in windows,
there, over the bench where you were sitting
hung the silk cocoon from the branch,
reminding you of your lock,
and everything will be repeated: you were sitting,
the Patriarch ponds were breathing
by the evening light of the plunged windows.
Maybe the fabulist's characters
made of wood and stone will come to life.
The monkey, the crayfish, the crow,
and the fox will crawl and fly up to the bench
to tell me that the whole day
you've been sad, sitting there
with your eyelashes simply
drooping.

I feel like a part of Amsterdam,
I live in it like a street painter.
A Rembrandt woman gives me coffee
and walks with me a night.

I rent a room on the deck of a yacht
steadily moving along the channels
and a Rubens heroine on the watch
will forgive me my last hour.

Thanks to the city for the part it played.
It's time to head for Antwerp, my bags
are light as I scatter salt on the medieval road,
and a gold coin flies skyward like a bird.

To the Master

To carry on, line by poetic line, toward the future
out of the ancient lodes of rich ore.
The grains are sparkling like mica,
like halos.

Young people herd to the cities driven
by the rhythm of pop music on CDs.
Thanks, old friend, for your wisdom,
for the unknown ridge that lies behind it,
for the image of the word that rises
from the depths of the soul

and stands up above the bustle, over the abyss,
over the lake shrouded by the mist at night.

A poet can be lured by a whirling dervish,
and by Nazareth, Visantya, and the Third Rome,
and the ancient statue looming behind
the burial mounds.

———————

The plot of our story is divided
into two apartments.
The light of our meetings
is wandering, and the black holes
will not shield the planets that circle.

We'll stand silently by the window
and see the city through rhyme.
The distance visible beyond the horizon,
in spite of the cold, is ours.

A thinly-knitted sweater.
Its collar is almost unfastened.
This is all, but God knows,
the look, that we caught by chance,

will sentence us by nightfall.

The night will be short,
the way long.
Anxiety, like a black thread
running down from the collar
will fill our days.
And the plane over the abyss
will shake in the turbulent air.
I don't know what's awaiting us.
An angel, somewhere by the Hudson River,
will stand by the blinking light.

Our story, our plot
is simple as two and two are four.
Why doesn't the light go out,
even if there is no light
in this ill-begotten world?

On the Melody of My Childish Books

Isn't the language of Aesop needed?
We weren't used to this until now.
Looking back at the door doesn't hide the fright
that will emerge in a state of anger.

We were tortured by this tale more than once.
Their comments aren't important now.
What is important is that thoughts
aren't forbidden and that every addressee is found.

Here is the book for children:
a child is reading letter after letter.
He doesn't know the truth between the lines,
the first lesson of reading out of school.

What is this country of fools?
Let the sound of its heels be inaudible,
let it not put on false smiles or
the inherited fear of sad eyes.

The Steppe and the Mountain

By Shomishbay Sariyev, translated by Ilya Bernshtein

to Mukhtar AUEZOV

G reat rivers and far-sounding winds
Carry the word to villages and *auils*:
The royal steppe and the proud mountain
Have come together in the hearts of Mukhtar and Rasul.
The glory of the earth is in their names
And in the fruits of their poetic garden—
The song of prairie grass in Mukhtar's art,
In Rasul's poems the songs of rockslides.
Glide down the trail of lines without a breath
Above the waterfall that falls like thunder.
The world is enchanted by the breadth of soul.
The world is charmed by the art of Rasul.

Through flames of dreams, beliefs, and myths,
Through the vast steppe, toward red horizons,
Shoulder to shoulder, right beside Rasul
Marches the high art of Mukhtar.
The palm is indivisible between the two,
The red ribbon of victory crowns them both.
Let the steppe bow before Rasul
And let the mountaintops greet Mukhtar.
Bend toward the spring and devoutly drink—
Without equals and without blemish
Are Mukhtar, who has sung the beauty of the steppes,
And Rasul, who has sung the proud mountains.

The pain of flowers and boundless fields is here,
The enamored whispers of a mountain *auils* …
The world is wonderful and proud and broad
In the art of Mukhtar
         and Rasul.

Time

Time
       is a swift tulpar,[1]
No faster steed
       lives on earth.
To fairytale delights
       in a wondrous land,
To my tomorrow
       it will deliver me.
Mountains and abysses,
         waters and flames,
My tulpar will overcome
          with ease.
This is what I dreamed of as a child
And I look at the world as a child even now.
Time knows neither doubts
           nor thirst.
It rumbles,
      splitting the silence in half.
Everything
      that I take from life,
One day
     I will give back
To life eternal
      twofold.
I tell myself,
      as I honor the living,
Pay what you owe to the people's songs!

---

1   Winged horse of Kazakh mythology.

Time!
     Onward, my time!
Into the future,
     my fairytale steed,
Into the future
     fly!

Everything in this world is eternal ...

Everything in this world is eternal—
Grasses in sunlight and dew.
In childhood lightly and freely
Everyone looks at life.
     What are sorrows to us!
     Before I loved anyone else
     I lived without even knowing
     That I lived for myself.
Cheerfully I lived, like a bird.
But the time, in my idleness, came
For me, also, to hurry
Toward my very first aim.
     The stubborn boy understood then
     That if your wings have grown strong
     You have to live to make mother
     Happy with you along.
Do your filial duty
And, to the end, to the end,
In grief and in joy remember
Your father, in battle who fell.
     It is about him that, at sunrise,
     The singer will weave a tale.
     We have grown up, his children—
     Now I'm a father myself.

My son bends like a sprig now,
Stretches out his hands and laughs.
A sacred vow I make now:
From mortal combat, if I have to,
I shall not flinch, for his sake.
      I honor friendship and courage,
      By honor and friendship I swear—
      I shall not forsake a friend in trouble
      Nor bow down before a foe.
Everything—obstacles, sorrows—
You shall overcome all with love.
Every drop of the sea
The sun gathers up in itself.
      Terribly raging, nature
      To him who passes through it
      Gives light. You must live for the people
      And for the Fatherland, poet!

There is no limit to grief …

There is no limit to grief
If grief has been made the rule,
If grief is as deep as the sea,
Always prepared for a storm.
Not alone did you suffer—
The whole people suffered as well.
And weary Vietnam struggled
For liberty and for truth.
The people fought
      with a stubborn belief
That together
      they would conquer grief …
The day arrived and over the land of Vietnam
Flared up a joyous dawn.
And for this peace on earth,
For which they had paid with blood,
Vietnamese mothers and children

Gave my homeland thanks.
Above Vietnam once again
            the sky is full of stars.
There is no more bondage,
            odious and bitter,
And the birds have come back
            and made nests
On the wounded, beloved earth.

Proposal

The Red Book of endangered species
Grows longer and longer
With every passing year …
There are fewer and fewer white swans,
Eagles,
Swift saiga antelopes,
Doe and deer …
There are fewer and fewer rare rainbow blossoms—
Their torn roots have withered …

Will the gray prairie grass,
The free beast
And the bird,
The rosy flower before dawn,
Vanish forever from the steppe?
Will nothing at all remain
But hot billowing dust?

For the sake of all things living
On Earth
Hearken to the chirping and the howling …
Lest you end up
Standing on cinders and ashes
Open this book of mourning:
It is high time to write down in this book,

In the name of life on our planet,
Those virtues which have always been held high
So that our children should not forsake them.
Let us write in it Love and Kindness,
The idea of Honor and the idea of Friendship,
Charity and Purity of heart—
The mighty weapon of Humanity.
Let us write in it all that we hold dear,
What is sacred in our hearts in any weather.
We will not sin against each other
If we bow down to Nature together.
The origin of all that is divine
Has been hidden in nature
Since the beginning of time …

He stood, leaning on crutches …

He stood, leaning on crutches,
Unnoticed by us, to the side,
And watched how the girls waltzed around,
Barely touching the ground.

By none recognized, by none comforted,
He did not try to hide his sadness.
He kept smoking, as if the smoke from his cigarettes
Could hide him from us like a curtain.

What heard he in his past, what came like a dream
Lit up by sonorous dawns?
Hidden from all, strangely he glanced
At the young men surrounded by girls.
Who and what might he be? From whence had he come? …
This horseman—we asked him nothing.
And not everyone saw that within his soul
Reigned a mournful autumn.

Not envy was displayed in his eyes
But a boundless sorrow growing colder.
And whence came the smile on his tightly shut lips?
From his heart and its mighty power.

He stood and he smoked … From all others apart,
O horsemen, he was nonetheless with us
And for him, as for anyone whose dreams have wings,
All roads in the world were open.

Nest on the Balcony

The passerby looks up, surprised by something—
The building looks
Like any other building.
But for some reason it has suddenly
Reminded him of his native *auil*
And of the wind that blows across the steppe so swiftly.

What can it be?
What is it that catches his eye?
The sunlight plays in the enormous windows,
But on the balcony is a swallow's nest
And the piercing cries of its babies.

The noise of crowded streets here never dies
And the piping of a chick here is not easy to notice.
I close my eyes and see the *auil* where I was born,
The smoke of the hearth, and under the roof a swallow.

I am moved—
Ready to break down and cry—
Before my eyes the years of my childhood have arisen.
Beneath this sky, from the beginning of time
Children and birds have grown up together.

Because a swallow on this roof has made her nest,
Under the roof one hears
The laughter of children.
She has brought goodness with her on her wings
And six—no fewer—little nestlings.

Meanwhile, the current of humanity swirls here
And life flows on
Broadly and boldly.
I look at the house where the swallow lives—
With her happiness has flown to this house also.

My land,
You are a fragile house for all.
May your warmth never diminish!
May carefree children's laughter ring and ring
And may a swallow come and build her nest here.

Steeds of the Steppe

Here come the tulpars,
Flying, flowing across the steppe
Like fallings stars …
Here comes the chestnut horse
Like fire's own brother,
The world spins backward in his wake …
Boldly the rider has released the reins
And with his legs presses the horse's sides.
Now like a flood
He flies
And overtakes the clouds up in the sky.
I know that slumbering honor will awake,
For the dream of the steppe
Is the dream of a flying steed.

Or a lightning's flight?
Sudden—
but far from accidental?
Everything in this world remains a mystery
And who—mysteriously—will understand this world?
What is not a riddle in this world eternal?
Glimmering stars?
Or a leaping shadowy form?
Everything in this world is mortal,
but also endless.
Now straining,
as in labor,
now freely,
In dead of night day hurries to be born.
What in the world is not a riddle?
Even at a funeral
We glimpse a light
that glimmers in the dark.
All of the world's mysteries are hidden
in the mystery of life
Planted on earth once like a spark.

Home

Just say: home …
Your heart will skip a beat.
There is no place like your paternal home.
Let the whole wide world lie at your feet—
Dearest of them all it stands alone.

Just say: home …
And light shines in your eyes,
As if you feel the touch of mother's hand!
After all, the hearth that's in her home
Is the origin of your Motherland!

Home and hearth—
Everything else must wait.

Song

This song was rocked by the hills
                like a babe in a cradle,
Blue mountains rocked it between their hands.
My ancestors sang this song, long and lonesome,
In it they melded and mixed their eternal grief.

This song rang out
        in the rolling and rushing streams in April.
Cattails picked up its tune and repeated it at dawn.
My ancestors sang this song, long and lonesome,
In it they melded and mixed their eternal grief.

The flutes of that song
        filled the winds of the deserts,
The waves of the lakes collected it sound by sound.
My ancestors sang this song, long and lonesome,
In it they melded and mixed their eternal grief.

The clusters of trees
        and the green pines of the mountains,
The trails and the roads of the nomads rocked it as well.
My ancestors sang this song, long and lonesome,
In it they melded and mixed their eternal grief.

O my steppe!
        The song of the earth is beating
In every heart—we have called that song fate.
My ancestors sang this song, long and lonesome,
In it they melded and mixed their eternal grief.

The world listens.
        Chasing away sorrows and troubles,
The song rings out—full of eternal love.
Could the steppe have become a dwelling for happiness
Had it not known and sung this song not?

Between morning and evening ...

Between morning and evening
        lies life's swift course.
What luck
    that we have been able to draw
Water from these two streams
        that flow and converge in one bed:
Sorrow and Cheer—
      these are the currents of life.
I am covered by the waves
        of these two rapid streams
That give me to drink
      now of grief, now of joy.
And if with one of these streams
I am drained from the source to the sea
Then the other raises me up
        clean and strong.
Thus, they roll on—
      two streams, between the same banks,
Leaving upon my lips
       now honey, now salt.
Now sweet prairie grass wafts its perfume
       from shore to shore,
Now it is drowned by *zhantak*,
        the camelthorn.
Two flavors has life
and two colors belong to time.
Now in a black cloud,
      night
spreads out its wings,
Now day
    swims into my waters,
         white as a swan.
And once again the foliage
       leafs through the book of Life.
And once again toward this book
       I stretch out my hand.

In a mountain current,
                    down a soft bed of sand,
Taking in both waters—
                    dark and light—
Between morning and evening
                    rushes
                    the river of life.

Afterword
The Expanding Horizons of Kazakh Literature and Culture

By Naomi Caffee
Ph.D. Candidate
Department of Slavic Languages and Literatures
University of California, Los Angeles

Now that the twenty-first century is fully a decade underway and we are already a generation removed from the breakup of the Soviet Union, authors and readers of Central Asian literatures are privy to new and expanding ideas about what constitutes a national literature. Nowhere is this more evident than in Kazakhstan, the region's multicultural, multilingual economic powerhouse, where the cultural landscape reflects the dynamics of the country's economic and sociopolitical development. Literature is no longer solely a state endeavor, as it was in Soviet times, but neither is it completely dependent on market forces. The advent of Internet publication and increased contact with Western financial sources has fundamentally altered the relationship between literary patronage, production, and reception. Of no less significance are the expanding geographical parameters of Kazakh literature, as Kazakhstanis become mobile, global citizens and forge new cultural ties to Western Europe, North America, and other areas of Eurasia. Moreover, within Kazakhstan itself we see a curious mix of a strengthening official national culture, spurred on by government efforts, as well as the diversifying effects of globalization, owing to Kazakhstan's increasing economic and strategic importance on the world stage. This, in turn, affects the content of literature, introducing new tropes, styles, genres, and devices. Therefore, perhaps paradoxically, Kazakh literature becomes more variegated even as state-supported avenues of national culture solidify.

With these developments in mind, we must first address the question: what *is* Kazakh literature today? Above all we should recall that the ethnonym "Kazakh" is distinct from the term "Kazakhstani," which refers to any citizen of the multicultural Republic of Kazakhstan. A similar disambiguation exists in Russia, where the modifier *russkii* (ethnically Russian) is contrasted to *rossiiskii* (of the Russian Federation). Thus, determining *who* is a Kazakh is a matter of personal and community identification, rather than top-down political designation. Indeed, Kazakh literature swells beyond the political and historical boundaries of the Republic of Kazakhstan, with ethnic Kazakh authors living and publishing throughout the Russian Federation and the CIS, Xinjinag Province in China, and even far-flung lands like the United States and Canada. For this reason, the contemporary Kazakh writer may have a wide range of experiences, languages, political affiliations, and cultural influences to draw from. This is not to mention the vast literary toolbox of mixed-heritage authors like Bakhyt Kendzheev, a Russophone émigré to Canada, whose work reflects the *toska po mirovoi kultury* ("longing for world culture") characteristic of early twentieth century Russian poets like Osip Mandelshtam. Within the Republic of Kazakhstan, as well, the distinction between Kazakh and non-Kazakh literature begins to blur, as authors from Russian, Kazakh, Ukrainian, Uzbek, Uyghur, Tatar, and a variety of other ethnic backgrounds converge on the Russophone literary scene. Therefore an increasingly pertinent question may very well be: what *isn't* Kazakh literature?

Another factor in the contemporary development of Kazakh literature is the physical and virtual mobility of Kazakh authors and their reading audience, which has served to strengthen international collaboration and contact. Particularly significant are the effects of online publishing and social networks, which provide an alternative to the model of the Writers' Union held over from the Soviet period. One example of such an entity is the Almaty-based cultural organization Musaget, which receives financial support from the Dutch NGO Hivas. Musaget members engage in a variety of activities: conferring literary prizes, holding readings and other literary events, publishing the online journal *Apollinarii*, and conducting master classes in literature. Musaget's activities have paved the way for the emergence of a "New Wave" of young authors such as Ilia Odegov, Tirgan Tuniants, Aigerim Tazhi, Marat Isenov, Vadim Gordeev, and Pavel Bannikov. Social networking sites such as Zhivyi Zhurnal (LiveJournal), Facebook, Twitter, Vkontakte.ru, and Stikhi.ru provide avenues for informal literary production, independent from institutional or market control. As a result, Kazakhs/Kazakhstanis now have fewer obstacles to access, interaction, and participation in literary life.

One result of the geographical and virtual expansion of Kazakh artistic life is the increasing visibility of Kazakh culture abroad. Musical groups, from the traditional folk ensemble Turan to the experimental rock trio Roksonaki, now embark on popular international tours. Likewise, artists from around the world travel to Kazakhstan for inspiration and collaboration with Kazakhstani colleagues. Nowhere is this more evident than in the 2005 epic film *Nomad,* based on the life of the legendary Kazakh warrior Abilay Khan. With Russian, Kazakh, and Czech-American directors, an Azerbaijani screenwriter, a Czech-American producer, and Kazakh and French financial backing, the film is a testament to the international appeal of Kazakh history and culture. Another example is the *Silent Steppe Cantata*, a joint project by the American composer Anne LeBaron, the Kazakh-American tenor Timur Bekbosunov, and the Kazakhstani Sary-Arka Folk Instrument Orchestra, which debuted in Almaty and Astana in 2011. With a libretto drawn from the works of Olzhas Suleimenov and other Kazakh writers, the piece offers a "portrait of a now renewed Kazakhstan, with its unusually rich natural resources, prevailing through hardship and endless difficulties with a spiritual unity inherent in the Kazakh ancient traditions."[1] In addition to such high-budget, high-profile endeavors, there are also numerous projects on the grassroots level. The Artpologist Project, a series of collaborative works by American artist Daniel Gallegos, features collaborations throughout Central Asia such as a graffiti arts festival held in conjunction with Almaty's first independent art gallery, Tengri Umai.

There is no doubt that the twenty-first century offers new social and spiritual realities to be explored in Kazakh literature and art. One issue that may gain greater consideration in the future is gender, since the literary field has so far been overwhelmingly male-dominated. Will economic changes affect traditional family and social structures, leading to the greater presence of women in Kazakh literary life? Another issue is the potential negative effects of globalization. Will mass "McCulture" stifle creativity and homogenize identity in Kazakh/Kazakhstani literature, or will the forces of globalization mold a multilingual, better-educated, tech-savvy, and politically conscious generation of writers?

For better or for worse, these issues increase the potential for a diversity of literary and artistic expression, which will captivate our attention for years to come.

---

1   Silent Steppe Cantata: Libretto, http://www.theoperaoftimur.com/ssc/The_Silent_Steppe/libretto.html

Glossary

aksakal—lit. white beard: elder, a venerable old man

apa, ata—a form of polite address, directed at one's elder (literally, mother/sister, and grandpa, respectively)

asik—a sheep's knuckle bone, used as a playing die

auil—settlement, village

baksi —bard, storyteller, musician

barkhan—dune, arc-shaped sand ridge

batyr—brave warrior, hero

burkit—the Golden Eagle, national bird of Kazakhstan

dastarkhan—a low table, a meal

jailau—summer pasture

jigit—a skilled young fellow

jut—an extremely snowy or icy winter, which makes it difficult for grazing animals to reach fodder, resulting in mass starvation and death

kafir—infidel

kamshi—whip

karasakal—lit. black beard, middle-aged man

kelin—a young married woman, bride, daughter-in-law

kese —small bowl used for drinking tea

kimiz—a traditional drink, made of fermented mare's milk

kiyak—giant ryegrass

kiyiz—felt, matted from sheep's wool, used as rugs, exterior covering of a yurt, etc.

kokpar—a sporting contest where two teams of horsemen vie for possession of a freshly slaughtered he-goat

korgan—hill or burial mound

kuman—a metallic or ceramic vessel made for holding and dispensing water or wine

kuyshi—a musician, specializing in the performance of the *kuy*, a traditional Kazakh musical form

mangal—a grill

papakha—a tall hat made from looped wool pile

paranja—a Muslim woman's dress, covering body and head

shalma—turban

shapan—an Oriental-style overcoat

shashlyk—a variety of shish kabob

shaytan—devil, Satan

shekpen—a heavy overcoat

Bibliography

This bibliography of selected publications on the modern culture and literature of Kazakhstan is designed to help scholars, students, and the general public in further study of this country. In the age of information technology it is a virtually impossible task to cover all publications and all sources in the limited space provided. There are several books available that comprehensively cover the culture of Kazakhstan, including the literature of Kazakhstan. In addition, there are several dozen websites that provide useful Internet links, bibliographies, and other data for further studies of Kazakhstan. At present, the single and most comprehensive bibliographical work is Yuri Bregel's three-volume *Bibliography of Islamic Central Asia,* published in 1995, which contains bibliographical references to thousands of books in English, Russian, French, German, Central Asian languages, and other languages as well. A group of scholars—Didar Kassymova, Zhanat Kundakbayeva, and Ustina Markus—prepared the *Historical Dictionary of Kazakhstan,* which was published by Scarecrow Press in 2012. This book is in fact a comprehensive reference source on Kazakhstan, including culture and literature of Kazakhstan, and has a valuable bibliography section.

Taking into the consideration that several books are available providing a comprehensive bibliography on the modern literature and culture of Kazakhstan, the editor chose the most prominent modern works found in major libraries in the USA, which can lead readers to other publications, giving priority to the most recent works.

Abazov, Rafis (ed.). *Green Desert. The Life and Poetry of Olzhas Suleimenov.* (Poetry translated by Sergey Levchin and Ilya Bernstein). San Diego, CA: Cognella, 2011.

Aktualniye problemi literaturovedenia, iskusstvoznania i folkloristiki na sovremennom etape. Materiali mezhdunarodnoi konferentsii. [Actual problems of literary criticism, cultural and folklore studies in modern period. Proceedings of an International Conference]. Almaty: Credos, 2011.

Allworth, Edward. *Soviet Asia Bibliographies: A Compilation of Social Science and Humanities Sources on the Iranian, Mongolian, and Turkic Nationalities, with an Essay on the Soviet-Asian Controversy.* New York: Praeger, 1975.

Auezov, Mukhtar. *Abai.* (Abridged). Moscow: Progress Publishers, 1975.

Bregel, Yuri, ed. *Bibliography of Islamic Central Asia.* Three volumes. Bloomington, Ind.: Research Institute for Inner Asian Studies, 1995.

Brzezinski, Zbignev and Paige Sullivan, eds. *Russia and the Commonwealth of Independent States: Documents, Data and Analysis.* New York: M. E. Sharpe, 1996.

Clarke, Kenneth and Mary, eds. *A Folklore Reader.* New York, A. S. Barnes, 1965.

Clayton, Sally Pomme, and Sophie Herxheimer. *Tales Told in Tents: Stories from Central Asia.* Frances Lincoln, 2005.

Curtis, Glen, ed. *Kazakhstan, Kyrgyzstan, Tajikistan, Turkmenistan, and Uzbekistan: Country Studies* (Area Handbook Series). Washington, D.C.: Federal Research Division, Library of Congress, 1997.

Elcin, Sukru, et al., eds. *Turk Dunyasi Edebiyat Metinleri Antolojisi* [The Anthology of the Literature of Turkic World]. Vol. 1–5. Maltepe, Ankara: Ataturk Kultur Merkezi Baskanlıggi, 2001–2004.

Frances Wood, *The Silk Road: Two Thousand Years in the Heart of Asia,* University of California Press, 2003.

Grant, Bruce. *In the Soviet House of Culture: A Century of Perestroikas.* Princeton University Press, 1995.

Gryaznov, Mikhail. *The Ancient Civilization of South Siberia.* London: Barrie and Rockliff, 1969.

Schnitnikov, B. *Kazakh-English Dictionary (Uralic and Altaic Series)*. London: Routledge Curzon, 1997.

Shoolbraid, G. M. H. *The Oral Epic of Siberia and Central Asia (Uralic & Altaic Studies)*. London: Curzon Press, 1997.

Smirnova N.S. *Istoria Kazakhskoi Literatury* [The History of Kazakh Literature]. Three volumes. Alma-Ata: Nauka, 1968–1970.